The

Old Whitaker Place

To Barbara —
with affection and
admiration,
Love,
David Crambers

The
Old Whitaker Place

a novella

By David Chambers

Miami University Press
Oxford, Ohio

Edited by David Schloss
Cover design by Madge Duffey
Book design by Dana Leonard

Library of Congress Cataloging-in-Publication
Data

Chambers, David, 1940-
The old Whitaker place / David Chambers ; edited
by David Schloss.
    p. cm.
ISBN 978-1-4507-0092-4
1. Older men--Fiction. 2. Dwellings--Fiction. 3.
Self-realization in old age--Fiction. 4. Vermont--
Fiction. I. Schloss, David, 1944- II. Title.
 PS3603.H353O43 2010
 813'.6--dc22
                                    2010001706

Printed on acid-free paper
in the United States of America

For John
and
for Jim Foxlow

Snow

The first flakes drift by my window, round and fluffy, unhurried, innocent appearing. But I am not fooled. They will accumulate, pile high, ruin my day. Last night the radio assured me the storm would pass to the north, but now they say it's coming this way, head on.

I brew some tea and open the back door for Roscoe. He trots down the steps, explores, pees, explores some more. I watch from the doorway. This is where I slipped last December. Roscoe and I stepped onto the porch before breakfast. Freezing rain had coated the boards during the night, then turned to snow and left a deceitful dusting. I took one step, slid, shifted forward and locked my knee to stop myself. I didn't stop. I twisted and fell, breaking my leg without hitting anything hard, a spiral fracture just above the ankle. Roscoe licked my face as I crawled into the house, this old Vermont farm house my great-grandfather built.

At seventy-nine, my bone cracked easily, healed slowly, kept me shut indoors for two months in a cast from the knee down. Worse than indoors:

confined to the first floor. Ben came up from Connecticut and stayed with me the first week. He carried the bed down from the second floor, gave me sponge baths, helped me in and out of bed during the night to pee. He came up every weekend after that until the cast came off. By the end, I was wild with humiliation and boredom.

Ben's my only child. I married late, divorced early. If he can get here through the snow, he'll be driving up today, as he does the first Saturday of every month. He'll arrive around noon and stay until late tomorrow. I'll make grilled cheese sandwiches for lunch, show him how self-sufficient his old man is. If he can get here.

He thinks I should move down to Connecticut. The last weekend I wore the cast, he said, "Dad, do you know where you'll go when you can't live on your own any longer?"

He phrased it kindly. He didn't claim I was already incapable. But I was offended anyway.

"I'm asking," he said, "because it's possible you could come live with me. I have that big extra bedroom."

"I appreciate the thought," I said.

He didn't press. He knows he couldn't stand living with me. I whistle to myself. I won't tolerate noises around me before breakfast. I have fixed ideas about what goes where: I'd rearrange his kitchen drawers, his medicine chest, his tool box. I've lived alone my whole adult life, if you don't count the four years with Ben's mother, which I don't, and if you don't count the holidays and summer vacations Ben spent with me, entire summers when he was in high school and college. I do count those. But mostly I've lived alone.

I couldn't live with Ben either for that matter. He's become a homosexual. He lives with a man named Morris, who moved in with him a few months ago. I haven't met this Morris person, but I'm sure that he and Ben do things I couldn't live in the same house with.

I glance out the window every few minutes. The snow is beginning to stick, at first just a gauze over the grasses, then covering them over, gathering in little clumps in the crotches of weeds. Out the front windows, I can no longer see the hills on the other side of the valley. Even the fir tree directly across the road is becoming fuzzy, dissolving. The land here rises behind the house, falls off in front. If the house were on skis and given a shove, it would slide across the road and, but for some trees, land in the White River a half mile east. If it wanted to, it could then float into the Connecticut River and head south through Massachusetts and Connecticut and on into Long Island Sound not far from where Ben lives.

I expected him to call this morning before he left. He's surely on his way by now. I dial his cellphone to warn him about the snow and have to leave a message, which is odd. He always leaves the phone on when he's driving. He'll call back, I'm sure, and when he does, I'll advise him to turn around, but he will insist on coming anyway. He's a good son.

It was only a few years ago he told me he was a homosexual. I suppose I should have suspected, since he was thirty-seven and not yet married, never mentioned girlfriends. But I was thirty-nine when I married, and I never talked to my parents about the women in my life. Also, he's tall like me and broad-shouldered — soft-voiced, but not at all swishy.

The snow falls faster now, smaller flakes but many more of them, a couple of inches on the ground in less than an hour. I've always been amazed that something as small and skinny as a snowflake can stack up so quickly. Like dog hairs under the bed. I take baby steps outside now whenever it flurries, hold onto the side of the house, carry the cell-phone Ben gave me for Christmas. You may think it strange, but I believe that his telling me he's a homosexual has made me even more wary of snow. I feel less manly now.

You know what I wish? I wish it were still November. I don't mind that the leaves would already be gone, that the wind would rise most afternoons, that whole days would fill with rain. No matter, I could still be outdoors. Early in the month I put the vegetable garden away, pull out roots, cover the beds with compost and leaf mulch. Roscoe and I take hikes in the woods, trudge up the meadow behind the house, admire the dried stalks of goldenrod and yarrow and mullein. All the browns of the rainbow. And then, to my sorrow, December stomps in. The snow that's falling now will hang around until March. I'll slog out the driveway to the mailbox each morning. I'll drive into the village for groceries and prescriptions. But I won't risk the woods or the high meadow. Mostly I'll huddle indoors, read, watch sports, play solitaire, stare out the window at the hillside, at its big blank movie screen of snow.

I call Ben again and leave a message urging him not to drive but to take the train. Amtrak runs one train up here every day. He can board in New Haven after lunch and reach White River Junction before dinner. Marilyn from Big Yellow Taxi could meet him at the station. As I hang up, I look at my watch and remember he's already on his way. It's too late to take the train. He's probably crossing into Massachusetts by now. Freezing rain may be covering the road. He could hit a patch of black ice and spin into a ditch, not be found until he's frozen solid. You read about accidents like that all the time.

Axel Grimmer just down the road almost froze right on his own place. I remember Axel whenever it turns cold. He reminds me of my grandfather Tom, for whom I was named. Axel went out to his barn one January afternoon, climbed into the loft and started pitching hay down for his cows. Halfway done, he lost his balance and fell through the scuttle, broke an arm on a railing and landed inside the feeder with one leg through the grating and his good arm wedged behind him. It was five degrees and he'd lost his cap in the fall. His ears ached, then went numb. The muscles in his neck and shoulders tightened up. He shivered so hard he was slamming his head against the side of the feeder. Lucky for him, his wife came home from work while he was still alive. By the time the ambulance arrived, he'd been trussed up in the feeder for a couple of hours. If he hadn't been out of the wind, he'd probably have died.

Ben could be in a ditch, the Toyota on its roof, Ben hanging upside down in his seatbelt, dead when the troopers find him. That's what this weather can do.

May God forgive me, but right after Ben told me he was homosexual I thought it would be a blessing if he died that sort of way, died as he drove home from here, before he'd told others in the family. It wasn't the sinfulness that upset me. I'm not particularly religious. And it wasn't just the unseemliness of the sex, though it is plenty unseemly. I think it was mostly his impudence, his willful decision to be strange and girl-like. Here he was, descended from countless generations of Whitaker men who did their duty — married, got women pregnant, supported a family, several generations in this very house. Yet he concludes that isn't good enough for him.

I'm not as addled about it anymore. Ben rarely talks about it these days and I don't mention it at all. I'd rather not have known, but now that I do, I've tried to understand. He gave me some books, and I read one — loose-thinking propaganda, it seemed to me—but I realize now that he didn't choose to be what he is. I'd love him either way, of course. He's my son. And I need his help. I need him now more than he needs me.

I look outside again, but cannot calculate how much snow has fallen. I want to tell Ben how deep it is when he calls. I take the yardstick and edge onto the porch to a spot that's sheltered from the wind. Five inches are on the ground already. I leave the measuring stick standing propped against the woodshed where I can see it from the window.

I used to like snow. When I was a boy, my family would come up here for Christmas. We lived in Concord then. If we had a storm like today's, Finnie and Ellen and I and my dad would build snow forts a snowball's throw apart. When the walls were finished, we'd all pack ammunition until we had enough for a raid. Then Finnie and I would charge Dad and Ellen with an armload, flinging and flinging until we barraged them into retreat, or vice versa. Back and forth, back and forth, until eventually Gram would shout "cocoa!"—snow by this time down the collars of our coats, inside our boots, hats lost, fingers stiff, laughing, oh lord how we'd laugh. I had no issue with snow back then.

The wind has picked up. The flakes stream sideways in a river flowing east. The yardstick tips over. After a few minutes the snow covers it. I'm sure you've heard the old saw that no two snowflakes look alike. Nonsense. Look for yourself. A billion snowflakes out there now. They all look the same.

If Ben comes up by train, I'll call Big Yellow Taxi to pick him up. No, right, he won't be coming by train, will he, because he's already on the road. But the train would have been a smart idea. I wish I'd talked to him in time. I've taken the Amtrak down a few times to see him. It isn't fast, but it's comfortable, dependable, safe. Last time he met me at the station and drove to Stony Hill, this old peoples' home I'd agreed to see, quite an expensive place. Everyone has his own apartment. A woman whose name I cannot recall, blonde hair, large breasts, took us around. Ben had arranged for us to stay for dinner, and just before we went in, the lady asked if I'd like to wash up. She pointed me to a bathroom, so I went in and took my shirt off to wash away the grime from the train ride. It took a while and then there's no towel, only one of these hot-air blowers. Ben rapped on the door and asked if I'm okay. Finally, I dried my armpits with toilet paper. I wouldn't live in a place that didn't have towels.

I still haven't heard from Ben and it's almost noon. I turn on the radio. They say they expect the storm to be followed by a mass of Arctic air swooping down from Canada. I imagine it arriving like a Zamboni. They also say that a totally different storm is moving up the eastern seaboard. I hope Ben's all right.

Last month, he told me his cousin Julie Kitchner is homosexual too. She's his mother's sister's daughter, his first cousin. He showed me a picture of her holding hands with another girl. My first thought was: a nice-looking young woman like her, what a shame. But my second thought was more constructive, an insight: that Ben's condition probably comes from his mother's side of the family.

The phone rings. I'm almost afraid to answer. It could be Ben calling from a snow bank. It could be the state police.

"Dad," he says. "It's me."

"Ben. Are you okay?"

"I got your messages, Dad. I'm at the office. Today is Friday. I don't come up until tomorrow."

I look at the clock. It tells me nothing, of course. But today isn't Friday, is it? It's Saturday. Isn't it Saturday? Apparently it's not. Ben keeps track of this sort of thing. He's an executive at a company that manufactures watches. "Oh, for some reason I thought you had Friday off," I say. I'm sure he can tell I'm lying. "Anyway, when you come up tomorrow, you'll need to drive cautiously. We have nearly a foot of snow already and it's still falling."

"A foot already?" he says. "Dad, did you know that we're supposed to get another storm down here starting late tonight? Mightn't it be wiser if I came up next weekend instead?"

"That's what I was going to suggest," I say, which isn't true, but is what I ought to have suggested. I want him here. I've been looking forward to it all week. He and I would play cribbage, talk politics, unclog the drain in the upstairs sink. "On the other hand," I say, "you could consider taking the train."

"Let's talk in the morning," he says. "If I can

make it to the station" — he lives twenty miles outside New Haven — "I'll come up."

"But you were right in the first place," I say, worrying that I'd sounded needy. "Why don't you just come next weekend?"

"If that's okay by you."

I hang up and look around. Suddenly, the house feels airless. I look out the front window. You can no longer tell the falling flakes from the already-fallen ones swirling off the roof. I can hear the wind in the chimney, feel it through some of the light switches.

Remember the Russian submarine that got tangled in cables on the ocean bottom? The crew was alive, but if they'd opened the hatch, they'd have drowned, and if they stayed inside, they'd have been asphyxiated. That's about the way I feel. Can't go out. Can't stay in. Well, of course, I can stay in if I have to. And I suppose I can get out, too. I can get out in the car. If the garage door will open. If I can back out of the driveway. If they plow the road.

Roscoe and I climb upstairs. We nap every day now for half an hour. Been doing it for seven years, ever since I sold the hardware store. I support myself on the railing, try to keep the weight off my bad knee. I know that if I move to Stony Hill, I can use an elevator. No pain using an elevator. No challenge either. Too many conveniences at Stony Hill. I couldn't look forward to clearing a drain.

Halfway up the stairs the power goes out and I have to squint in the winter half-light to find my way to the bedroom. I won't be able to set the alarm, but I don't care. Today I just want time to pass. I lie in bed listening to the wind, trying to figure out why Ben would choose to spend tomorrow with Morris rather than with me, even though it's my weekend.

More than two hours later—I hardly ever sleep this long during the day—Roscoe and I descend the stairs. The power's come back on, at least temporarily, but I cling to the railing anyway because I'm groggy and the steps are narrow and steep. Even Roscoe comes down slowly. He's seven, a Springer spaniel, somewhat overweight, not a pup anymore.

In the living room, I climb onto the exercise bicycle. I'm supposed to pedal every day for half an hour for the sake of my knees and heart. I don't, of course. I pedal only when I want to, and I happen to want to today, because it will kill some time, help me wake up. I watch television while I pedal. Since it's Saturday afternoon, I expect to watch football. But, of course, when I click on the set, I find yet again that it's not Saturday at all, so I watch a cooking show where this yakety-yak woman makes a casserole of the sort that Ben would have made if he had come. When she finishes, she pulls the dish out of the oven and tilts it toward me. "Voilà," she says. "Voilà yourself," I say, and dismount the bicycle, turn off the TV.

I notice that it's totally silent. The wind has died. The shutters no longer rattle. I look out the window but can't see much because it's getting dark. I open the back door and put my shoulder against the storm door to push away a drift. Roscoe and I stand in the arc of cleared snow. The moon lights the hillside. The snow, which has stopped completely, has been blown into ridges. It looks like the Himalayas. Majestic. Ominous. The moonlight is fluorescent, ice cold. I close the doors, pull the curtains.

Not much later, the phone rings.

"Dad," says Ben, "it's me again."

"Has it started snowing down there?"

"I don't know. I'm not down there."

"Where are you?"

"I'm on my way up to see you."

"That's great." He must have picked up on my disappointment. I'm embarrassed but relieved.

"Morris is with me. We thought we'd drive up during the gap between storms."

"Morris?" I've never told Ben he could bring Morris here. "I thought you weren't coming until next weekend."

"We're near Brattleboro."

"You and Morris."

"You haven't eaten, have you, Dad? We're bringing dinner. We'll be there in an hour or so."

I hang up. I walk around the kitchen. I was hungry ten minutes ago, but now I have no appetite. My quiet weekend, shot.

I knew he'd bring Morris sometime, but I'm not prepared for it today. They'll want to sleep in Ben's room, just a single wall between them and me, a wall so thin you can hear a fart through it. If the second storm swerves this way and dumps more snow, the three of us will be marooned together all weekend. Three of us alone in that Russian sub on the bottom of the ocean.

I feel tight in the chest. I open the back door and the storm door, take deep breaths, pull the cold air deep into my lungs. I gaze at the moonlit hill and am startled, struck dumb. I don't have my glasses on, but it looks as if the hill itself is creeping this way, inching like a glacier. On second look, I'm certain there is movement on the hillside, but only at the very top. A puff of snow flies off the crest. Snowballs begin rolling toward the house. I hear a distant rumble, hear it clearly. It's an avalanche. I slam the door and race for the stairs, shouting for Roscoe. Flashing before my eyes are news clips from Pakistan or Nepal or someplace, just a year or two ago: whole villages buried under snow and ice and boulders and splintered trees, old men standing on snow mounds looking down hopelessly, their wives and grandchildren buried thirty feet beneath them. It's coming with a roar now. It sounds like the Amtrak. I cringe in the bedroom doorway, holding Roscoe's collar.

Nothing happens. Nothing at all. The booming recedes and disappears. At last, I recognize what it was: the snow plows, two of them clearing the road. You can hear them from a long way off. Of course that's what it was. I've heard them a thousand times. Snow plows, for god's sake.

I try to think. I was upset about something before the avalanche. Something about Pakistan, was it? No, something about Ben.

I sit on the window seat in my bedroom. It's quiet again. I'm shaking a little, the back of my shirt drenched. I'm panting from running up the stairs. My calves ache. I'm ashamed of mistaking the plows for a snow slide. The road's been cleared. Ben will arrive soon. Ben and what's-his-name.

I could call them back, say I've gotten sick. But they've come all this way. I will have to be civil.

I help Roscoe up onto the seat beside me. I talk to him about the snowstorm and become anxious all over again, so I cast about for another subject. I talk about summer, about next summer, about my plans for the garden. I will plant tomatoes again, of course—more plum tomatoes than I did last year, and more basil. And cherry tomatoes, too. They're so full of flavor. Tomatoes taste better when you've grown them yourself. Ben and I spent Labor Day weekend simmering a dozen quarts of tomato sauce. We do it every summer. I'll take a jar out of the freezer for this evening. That's what I'll do. They'll be hungry when they get here. We can defrost it in the microwave, have it with spaghetti for supper, Ben and me and Morris. That's his name, Morris. Morris. Morris. Morris. I mustn't forget.

I chatter on about the garden, about manure and slugs and aphids, until Roscoe barks and I hear Ben's honk as he pulls into the driveway. Roscoe bounces down the stairs, too swiftly for his own good. I follow slowly, holding onto the railing. As I descend, I can see into Ben's room. I'll wear ear-plugs if I have to.

On My Land

My knees ache, of course, but when Morris asks how I'm doing, I turn and salute. I'm too out of breath to speak. It's summer now. He and Ben and I have zigzagged up the hill behind the house, not up the steepest way, but plenty steep enough. I've climbed to the top a thousand times, but not since I broke my leg. I should have brought a flag to plant at the ridge line to celebrate my achievement. Instead, I take a pee, an old man's dribbling pee to mark my territory. I own two hundred acres here, two hundred six to be exact, all but a few too sharply pitched to plow or build on, not worth much as timber. Scraggly, rock-strewn, dear to my heart.

I rest every few minutes, drink lots of water on this warm morning. Ben and Morris accommodate themselves to my halting pace. We'd be even slower if Roscoe had come along. He's limping these days. Beyond the ridge, Ben suggests bending to the right, onto a smaller path that leads to the meadow where the property ends. Fine with me. I'm happy surveying my domain.

The boundary line is partway down the meadow,

an odd place for a boundary, but the original lots were drawn in the eighteenth century by Massachusetts men who never ventured up to look. A century later, right after the Civil War, my great-grandfather bought our parcel for three dollars an acre, and at his death passed it to my grandfather. Both men were farmers but neither ever hayed the remote field where we're headed now. It's more than half a mile from the house. They let the farmer who owned the lower half use it for his stock. Dermott was his name. Lemuel Dermott.

I see light through the trees ahead. If the maple saplings haven't grown too tall, we'll have a long view to the north and west—of receding hills and some working farms, and to the left Killington and Pico, the highest peaks in this part of the state. It's early June, but they'll still have snow near the summits. I don't mind snow at a sufficient distance.

The trail widens at the end, like the mouth of a river, and as I step into the sunlight, I am frozen in my tracks, not by the sight of Killington, but by a house, one of these log cabins made of naked, barkless trunks. Less than a hundred feet in front of us. On my land. Someone has dug a foundation and erected a house. A driveway slices across the hillside, then disappears into the woods at the edge of the field. A pickup truck squats on the gravel. People live here. On my land.

"What is this?" says Ben, as amazed as I.

"You didn't know it was here?" Morris asks.

"Dad," says Ben, "isn't this your part of the field?"

I'm still staring.

"Dad?" he says.

I'm trying to comprehend. How did it get here? Who would have the gall to build on land that wasn't theirs? For that matter, who would want a house way up here anyway? There's a view, I grant you that, but in winter you'd have to plow for a quarter mile just to get down to the dirt road below, and the dirt road itself might not be passable. I feel disoriented, as if I'd climbed upstairs to find something and can't remember what it was.

"Hello," someone shouts from the direction of the house, and after a moment I spot a young woman waving from a window on the second floor.

"Hello," Morris shouts back.

I'm still speechless.

"We live on the other side of the hill," Ben shouts. "We didn't even know there was a house here."

I find my voice. "Tell her it's my land," I say.

"Shhh, Dad," says Ben. "Let's take this slowly."

"This is my land!" I shout at her.

"Then we're neighbors," she says. "I'm Debby Potter, and this is Megan." A child's eyes peer over the window sill.

Ben puts a hand on my shoulder. I brush it off. "You don't understand," I shout. "Your house is on my land!"

That shuts her up. She leaves the window and she and the girl reappear out the back door with a stocky man, her husband I assume, and a black dog three times the size of Roscoe. I start down the hill toward them. The dog snarls.

"I'm Dick Potter," the man says. "And you are?"

Ben has followed me, grabs me by the arm, pulls me to a halt. "Dad," he whispers, "screaming isn't going to help."

I struggle to free my arm, but he holds firm.

"Stop," he says.

I cannot look him in the eye.

"You stay here. I'll go talk to them."

He releases my arm. "I'm Ben Whitaker," he says loudly to the fellow squinting from the porch. "And this is my father, Tom Whitaker, and my friend Morris Berman."

Ben strides down the hill and shakes hands with the man and his wife. He has a firm grip, but with that quaver in his voice, he's not imposing enough. Morris is even skinnier than Ben, and shorter. Definitely not imposing. I should be the one talking. I could still go down, of course, but I feel dizzy. What I really need to do is sit, though if I do, Morris will have to help me up, and they'll be watching. As it is, the man and his wife dart glances at me, so I stand erect, feet apart, arms folded, wobbling just a little.

Ben steps off the porch and starts back toward us. The man slams the door. I can see the wife looking fearful through the glass.

"What did you say to them?" I ask. "Did you say I was old and crazy?"

"Of course not. I said we think this part of the meadow belongs to us and that either they or we have made a mistake."

"They or we?" I say. "They or *we?*"

"They claim the property line is at the top of the field just into the woods. They say there's flagging along the boundary."

"Anyone can flag," I say, my voice rising. "Listen, when the Dermotts owned the lower part of the meadow, Lemuel wanted to buy the top part from Grandfather, but Grandfather wouldn't sell. Dermott wouldn't have tried to buy from Grandfather if Grandfather hadn't owned it. Am I right?"

"You've got a point," says Ben.

"I think I'll go down and tell them that," I say, turning around.

"No," says Ben. "We're going back to the house. We need to talk to Larry Stillman first." Ben turns me toward home, cradling my elbow as the three of us work our way back to the top of the meadow. I don't resist. I'm still woozy. Larry and, before him, his father Harold have been the family lawyers for fifty years.

"Over there," Ben says, as we enter the woods, "a piece of the flagging." Someone has tied a strip of plastic ribbon, bright orange, around a nearby maple. I'm surprised I didn't notice it when we came the other way, but when I step off the trail to remove it, Ben steers my elbow ahead.

We pick our way down the steep pitch on the other side of the ridge, and I find, as ever, that down is easier on the heart but harder on the knees. Ben shifts from walking beside me to hovering close behind. The trail crosses other trails blazed by my father and me in the 1950s. We made them for my grandmother after my grandfather died. Most mornings, except in the worst of winter, Gram pulled on her Wellingtons and hiked into the woods to check on the birds.

"Buck up, Tom," says Morris, startling me. None of us has been talking. "I'm sure it will all work out."

My forebears were stewards of the land. They built the house and barn, kept them in good repair, kept the meadow open above the house. They fought gypsy moths and tent caterpillars, land speculators, moles and groundhogs, even bears. And me? Look at me. An intruder builds an entire house in the far field, and I didn't even know.

"The Potters don't seem like bad sorts," Ben says. "I'm sure they thought it was their land."

"So?" I say.

"I just mean that we shouldn't deal with them as if they were criminals."

"I'll be nice as long as they remove the house."

He and Morris exchange glances. We're all quiet again until we stop for a rest on the trunk of a downed pine.

"Do you remember," says Ben, "the story you used to tell about when you lived in Concord, coming out into the parking lot after a movie and finding that couple petting in the back seat of your car? You threw open the door and the girl had her blouse open and burst into tears. The guy thought you were a security guard and offered you ten dollars not to arrest them. And then it turned out it wasn't your car after all."

Morris laughs, but I don't. "She was right to have been embarrassed, fooling around like that in public."

"But the point is it wasn't your car. We need to be careful."

"The land is mine, Ben. The house is on my land. I should run them off with a shotgun, that's what I should do. That's what my great-grandfather would have done." I lift myself to my feet, raising my arms toward the unresponsive sky, gaze across the hills toward New Hampshire, admirable New Hampshire, whose land-loving citizens respect the property rights of others. "Damn it, Ben. I'll call the sheriff when we get back to the house and have him evict them."

Over dinner, Ben asks, "Do you want to call Larry Stillman, or do you want me to?"

"I should do it," I say.

"That would be fine."

"Or you could," I say. I don't like telephones.

I'm exhausted, but when I climb into bed, I'm unable to sleep. I can't get the Potters out of my head. I'm haunted about letting down my father, my grandfather, and my great-grandfather, my whole lineage. For all I know, the Potters may be planning an entire subdivision. I'll bet they found out I broke my leg and thought I'd never climb up and see what they were up to. I should wake Ben, tell him that Larry Stillman needs to get onto this right away.

After breakfast, I pester Ben until he dials Larry at home. It's Sunday but I don't care. This is critical. Quietly, I pick up the other receiver and listen. Larry is surprised by what Ben reports. He's glad to help, but we'll have to wait until he finishes a trial that starts in a few days. As soon as he can find time, he'll trace the chain of title for both the Potters' land and ours and take a trip out to the meadow. "There's possible good news here, Ben," he says. "Your dad could end up with a windfall. If he owns the land, then he owns the house, because the house is a structure permanently affixed to the land. The Potters can take their furniture, but your dad will own the house."

I can't keep quiet any more. "I don't want the house."

"Well, hello, Tom," says Larry. "I didn't know you were on the phone."

"Neither did I," says Ben.

"I want you to force Potter to put the land back the way it was," I say.

"I'll do the best I can," says Larry.

"That's all we can ask," says Ben.

"That's not good enough," I say.

"Tom," says Larry, "I need to warn you that boundary disputes bring out the worst in some people. And this one has the potential for becoming especially nasty. Most are just disagreements about a fence. I've never heard of someone building an entire house on the wrong land."

In late afternoon, Ben and I sit down to play cribbage. Morris is outside, weeding the garden, which I can't keep up with anymore and which he claims he likes to do. He's quite a knowledgeable gardener.

As Ben shuffles the cards, he clears his throat. "Dad," he says, "can I ask you a few questions?"

I nod.

"Morris and I have been talking, and he's helped me think more clearly. Tell me, what plans do you have for the upper part of the meadow?"

"Plans?"

"Yes, were you planning to build something there yourself?"

"Of course not."

"So, do you have some other plan for it?"

"I don't like where this conversation is going."

"Just stick with me. How much land are we talking about anyway, in the upper part of the meadow?"

"Quite a bit," I say, on my guard. "An acre and a half. Maybe more."

"Let's say it's two acres, and let's say you really do own it." He leans toward me over the table. "Right now, you own a house and barn and two hundred six acres. Taken together, they'd probably sell for several hundred thousand dollars, don't you think?"

"I don't know. Probably. They're not for sale."

"I understand. But do you think they'd be worth any less if you sold the house and barn with two hundred four acres rather than with two hundred six?"

"That is not the point, Ben."

"Well, what exactly is the point, Dad? The meadow is so far from the house it might as well be in Canada. You have no plans to use it. And getting rid of it wouldn't reduce the value of the rest of the property. If you sold it to the Potters for even a few thousand dollars, it would be like free money. It could pay for new storm windows."

"What you're trying to tell me is you think I should sell. Is that it?"

"Just that small parcel, yes."

"You're not a real Whitaker. A real Whitaker wouldn't suggest such a thing. Was this Morris's idea?"

"No, it was mine."

Late in the day Ben and Morris return to Connecticut, and for a second night I have trouble sleeping. For all I know, Potter may have altered the deeds in the town clerk's office. He might even hire someone to rub me out.

Finally, I give up and turn on the lights. Roscoe, lying next to the bed, raises his head in puzzlement, and I deliver a homily to him about people who encroach and people who steal, about claim jumpers and cattle rustlers in the Old West, about Germany invading Poland, about Argentina invading those little islands in the South Atlantic. My stomach churns.

For reasons I cannot fathom I also keep thinking about Ben's mother Claudia, as if she has something to do with this. Eventually, it dawns on me.

When she and I married forty-some years ago, she and her two little girls moved into my house — not this house, the house in Concord where I was living then. Right off, she acted as if she owned the place. I'd bought it just a few years before, planted a vegetable garden, added maple paneling to the little den. I wanted my new stepdaughters to feel at home, of course. They would share the second bedroom. I was prepared for that. But Claudia decided each of them needed a room of her own, so I gave up my den, and one day while I was at work, she painted the paneling a greeny sort of yellow. Kitty-litter yellow I called it. Within a few years, every other room had been repainted some female color, and she'd bought a new sofa for the living room that was covered in a blossomy pattern no man with self-respect would sit on. She complained when I ate popcorn on it. After a while, it didn't seem like my house anymore. Ben, who was born a year after we married, had just turned three. Finally, I packed up and left, nearly broke — gave Claudia almost everything and walked away.

At the general store, after no sleep at all, I ask Andy the owner if he knows a fellow in the neighborhood named Potter.

"You mean Dick Potter," he says.

"A husky fellow," I say.

"Everyone knows Dick."

I nod.

"He heads the road crew for the town now. His wife Debby teaches grade school in Thetford, or used to."

"They've built a house up near me," I say, matter-of-factly.

"I heard they did most of the work themselves. Have you met them?"

"Just to say hello."

"Oh, you'll like them."

I nod noncommitally. I respect Andy, trust his judgment, but he needs to learn a thing or two about the Potters' character.

All day I feel antsy. I can't think about anything else. It's a stone in my shoe. When lawyers tell you they'll do something as soon as they can, they mean they'll do something as soon as they get around to it. I can't wait that long.

At bedtime, I take some sleep medicine the doctor gave me when I broke my leg, and just after dawn, after a decent sleep, I get into the car with my camera. Through the kitchen window, Roscoe watches grumpily as I pull out of the driveway. I head north and turn onto the dirt road that leads to the Potters'. I haven't ventured up here in quite some time. I pass one house shortly after the turn and nothing else until I reach a new driveway. But I don't turn in. I park around the next bend.

Here's my plan. I'll hike through the woods to the meadow and then up the meadow's western edge until I find the pile of stones my grandfather and Lemuel Dermott erected to mark the corner of our land and his. It's the starting point for the boundary line that runs across the meadow. An old-fashioned cairn is what it is. I don't know why I didn't think of it when we had the lawyer on the phone. At the top of the cairn is a rock about the size of a cantaloupe. Dermott or Grandfather painted it red, and Dad and I repainted it sometime in the sixties. I'll take pictures of it. The Potters are probably still asleep, but even if they aren't, they won't see me from the house. The meadow's wide and the woods are dark.

I step cautiously across a ditch into the woods, proceeding slowly, a concession to knees and sciatica. Despite the perils, I find myself whistling. I pass the foundation of the old Dermott place. The house has long since tumbled in upon itself, abandoned in the 1930s, when the Dermotts, like so many other Vermonters, walked away, bankrupt and demoralized, unable to pay their loans or their taxes, unable to find a buyer at any price. The woods near here hide many old foundations. You can spot them by the day lilies still blooming around them, heartlessly, in midsummer.

When I emerge at the lower edge of the meadow, I proceed to the right until I reach the line of woods turning up, the line that will lead to the cairn. The trees are mostly evergreens, white pine primarily, dead lower limbs poking out in all directions. I pick my way through, break off small branches to get by, take my time. I stop to drink water from my canteen. I watch for slippery rocks, keep myself parallel to the edge of the meadow. To my left, across the field, the sun is rising above the trees.

When I was in high school, I used to visit my grandparents in the summer. I'd take off from the back porch of the house, run up the hill to the ridge, through the woods to this meadow and on down to the dirt road, then all the way home. I can't run anymore, but, by God, I feel some of that old gusto. This is going to be a good day.

Over the brow of the hill, I begin to see the upper half of the log house. More and more of it appears. It doesn't look any better from the front than it did from the back. I keep a sharp eye out for the cairn, but don't see it yet. Potter may have destroyed it.

And then I spot it, almost bump into it. It's no longer as tall as it was, at least not as tall as I recall, but the red rock still rests at the top, like the ball at the top of a barber pole. The house is above me, right where I thought it would be: on my land.

I take the camera from my pocket, and, in the early morning light, take shots from several angles, the most crucial of which is from below the cairn, with the house looming in the background. I squat for the triumphant shot, ignoring the pain shooting up my leg. As I click the shutter, I hear a bark and, looking up, see the Potters' dog bounding toward me, roaring. He's the color of a panther and the size of a pony. I try to stand, but my knees won't cooperate. I see his teeth now, his fangs, the spittle at the corner of his mouth, and with one desperate effort to rise, succeed instead in falling on my side. A wise maneuver, it turns out. I lie immobile, too shaken to move. Blue-edged black blobs bobble behind my eyelids. The dog doesn't attack. I can feel his breath as he sniffs my face. After a while he seems to lose interest, concludes, I suppose, that I am inedible, ambles away.

The ear that hit the ground is ringing. In fact my whole head is ringing. I'm cold, especially my legs, which seem to be shivering. I can't quite feel them, but I hear them rustling leaves and pine needles. I'm holding something in my hand, but the hand is pinned beneath me. I feel myself stiffening all over and realize that I have to try to stand. I roll onto my stomach, freeing my trapped arm, finding that what I'm clutching is a camera, but not understanding why. Woozily, I stuff it into my pocket, struggle to my knees and crawl to a nearby stump. I push myself erect, one leg at a time, teetering much like Roscoe when he first gets up. Where is Roscoe, by the way?

"Roscoe," I call, not remembering whether he was with me. I look around but do not see him. What I see is the red rock. Ah yes. That's why I'm here. That's why I have the camera. I lean against the nearest tree until I feel steady enough to move on.

Descending the hill takes twice as long as climbing up. When I look down, I see low limbs I might impale myself on. My goal is much less exhilarating than before. I'm no longer gathering evidence. I'm simply trying to make it down alive. But I do make it, by holding onto branches, by resting on boulders and fallen trees, by reminding myself how awkward it would be to be caught trespassing upon those who've trespassed against me. I reach the car, after nearly slipping into the ditch by the edge of the road.

"I did it," I say aloud. I'm grimy and bruised, but I did it. Don't mess with Tom Whitaker.

I drive directly to the pharmacy in the village, ask them to have the film developed as soon as possible. I also buy some aspirin and swallow a few right there in the store, then drive home still amazed at my achievement. I've climbed Everest. I've found the Holy Grail.

I do not notice the car parked in my driveway until I start to turn in. The driver sticks her head out the window. I get out of the car, just as she does.

"Mr. Whitaker. I was just coming to see you."

"Yes?"

"I'm your neighbor, Debby Potter. Can we talk for a few minutes?"

The enemy.

"I shouldn't be here," she says, "but I'm so upset by all this. I haven't been able to sleep."

"I can understand."

Wait until she sees my photographs.

"Yesterday afternoon we had a surveyor out. He measured everything against the descriptions in the deeds, and it turns out our house really is on your land. I still can't believe it. He also found the pile of rocks with the red stone."

"Yes." I can't think of anything else to say. I'm

relieved by their quick surrender, but also thinking, damn, I climbed that hill for nothing.

"Are you all right, Mr. Whitaker?"

"Just a little tired. I've been for a hike."

"Good for you." She offers me her arm. I ache everywhere. As we climb the front stairs, I make sure she cannot see my grimace.

"We were taken in by the sellers. Or maybe they were taken in by the people who owned before them. We believed them when they showed us the orange flagging up at the top."

I lower myself into the rocker on the front porch.

"May I sit?" she asks. I nod. She sits in the other rocker.

"It turns out that the front of our house is about ninety feet inside your boundary."

"That sounds about right."

"So the reason I've come is to ask you, to beg you really, to sell us a small parcel right around the house."

I shouldn't be talking to her now. I need rest. I need more aspirin. But she keeps talking, and I try to concentrate.

"Dick and I put in so much effort. We did the framing ourselves, the wiring too, most of the plumbing. It breaks my heart just to think about it." She looks at me, beseeching.

I have to be strong. "The land has been in my family for a very long time," I say.

Her expression doesn't change.

"My great-grandfather bought it in 1866. He

passed it on to my grandfather. None of it's ever been sold off. Not one square inch."

"I see."

I sit like a cairn.

"We're not talking about very much," she says. "We don't need all the way to the edges of the meadow, just a little space all around the house, half an acre or so altogether."

"I'm sorry," I say, "but it's not for sale."

She closes her eyes, then opens them. "I shouldn't have come," she says. I fear she's about to cry, but she doesn't. She looks me in the eye until I cannot look back any longer.

"We could pay you well for it. We bought title insurance for just this sort of problem. And, if the insurance won't pay, we have some savings. Dick and I have talked about it. He doesn't know I'm here, but I think we could come up with several thousand dollars."

"It isn't a matter of money."

She sits, without stirring. I think I should stand to signal that the conversation is over, but my knees won't let me rise with any authority.

Axel Grimmer drives by and I wave. I'll bet he wonders who this good-looking young woman is sitting here with me.

She shifts in her chair, as if her back were hurting. I find myself watching her hands, which lie limp in her lap, and see that she has a bulge in her abdomen. It isn't fat. Fat doesn't sit that way. I'll bet she's pregnant. She's quite a pretty woman, a little on the

hefty side, but the solid sort I've always appreciated. Not overweight. Solid like my grandmother.

We sit without speaking.

"I guess I'll be going," she says, pulling herself
out of the rocker.

As she starts down the porch steps, I feel this idea
welling up inside me. "Wait," I say.

"Yes?"

"I might consider renting."

"Renting," she says. "I hadn't thought about renting."

I hadn't either actually. It just came out of my
mouth.

"Yes," I say. "Some sort of long-term lease."

"Would that work?" she says, stepping back up
to the porch.

"I'd still have the title, but you could use the
land."

I have lots of ideas I come to regret. At the moment, I don't know what I'm getting myself into. I
wonder what my grandfather would think.

She looks uncertain. "We'd have to agree on how
much the rent would be. So much a month, I suppose."

My grandfather always let the Dermotts grow
hay on the upper part of the meadow. He didn't
charge them, but it was like a rental. He was a good
man, my grandfather, a stern Vermont farmer who
put two sons and a daughter through college and
represented our town in the legislature for twenty-some years. I feel magnanimous, gaseous, a bit
out of control. "I wouldn't worry too much about

the rent," I say. I sit for a minute to collect my thoughts. She doesn't say anything more, waiting for me. "Here's my proposal. I'll lease you the part of the meadow I own, up to the orange flagging."

"All the way up?" she says.

"For as long as there's a house on the land."

"Do you mean it?" she says.

"I wouldn't joke about something like this."

"That would be excellent. That would be so excellent."

"And the rent will be one hundred dollars a year."

"You mean a month?"

"No, a year."

Suddenly, just when she ought to be overjoyed, she looks apprehensive. "Mr. Whitaker, perhaps you should talk this over with your son and get his advice. Do you think he will be okay with this idea?" I can see that she's looking at the mud that's caked in my hair.

"Do you think I can't make this decision myself?"

She bursts into tears. "No, no. I don't think that. I don't know. Oh dear, I think I'm the one who's not thinking clearly. It's just you're being so generous."

"Listen," I say, trying hard to look dignified, trying hard to look sane. I can't remember her first name. I can't remember her last name either. "I said before that this wasn't a matter of money. I meant what I said."

"I know. I know," she says, blowing her nose into a tissue. "Thank you very much." After a few minutes full of more thank yous, she gets up to leave. She shakes my hand, and just before she heads down the steps, kisses me on the top of my head.

"Goodbye, Mr. Whitaker."

"Wait just a minute. There is one other condition."

She stops. "Yes?"

"Each year you have to deliver the one hundred dollars in person."

Storm Windows

My hand has shrunk, all except the swollen, knobby knuckles. The rest has shriveled like a baked apple, the skin spider-webbed and creased. And look. Liver spots everywhere, yellow-brown spots, toast-brown spots, mostly round, but some in the oddest shapes: a hunkering rabbit, a baseball cap, a lima bean. And the veins that run between the knuckles down to the wrist. They've popped up like mole trails, pale blue, under skin as thin as tissue paper. I'm becoming transparent.

"Dad, are you listening?"

"What?" We are sitting at the kitchen table, finishing breakfast. It's springtime. Ben's here for the weekend. Morris sometimes comes with him, but not this time.

"We were talking about Aunt Ellen."

"Oh, yes." Ellen. My sister.

"I said I'm going to see her next week when I'm in Detroit."

"Yes, please give her my regards."

"And I said that when I see her, I plan to tell her about Morris moving in with me, so I wanted to know if you had ever gotten around to telling her that I'm gay."

The doctor said that liver spots have nothing to do with the liver. They come from long exposure to the sun, merit badges of an outdoor life. They're not cancerous. The cancer ones look different.

"Well, have you?"

"He hasn't been living with you that long."

"Almost two years."

"It's never come up, Ben. She doesn't call that often, you know."

He snorts, looks the other way.

"Will you be telling Bruce, too?" I ask. Ellen's husband, retired baseball coach, snowmobiler.

"No, just Ellen. She can tell Bruce if she wants to. And Proctor and Rachel."

Their children. Proctor's an airline pilot, serious golfer, father of four. Rachel's a mortgage broker.

I wait until Ben turns his head back. "I wish you wouldn't say anything to Ellen."

"Why?"

"I don't think she'd understand. I think it would just upset her."

"Dad, Ellen was a dancer in New York before she married Bruce."

"Well, Bruce won't understand. I'm sure of that."

"What exactly is there to understand?"

"Or Proctor either. Or Bethanne." Proctor's wife, frosted hair, thin lips.

Ben picks up yesterday's newspaper. I stir my coffee, flick some crumbs off the table. Of course, I realize that this isn't just about Ellen. It's about me, too. But Ellen really is sensitive, prone to worry. She's always thought so highly of Ben. I've boasted about how well he did in college, how successful he's been at work. I've even mentioned girlfriends who didn't exist. She's old now, too, almost as old as I am, and Bruce is older than either of us. Leave them in peace, I say.

Ben turns pages noisily. I get up and rinse the breakfast dishes. After a while, he turns pages more quietly, then folds the paper and nods. "Dad, what do you say we take out the storm windows and put in the screens?"

"Now?"

"Why not?"

"Yes, why not," I say.

I believe he has just agreed not to say anything to Ellen.

Outside it's balmy, blue-skied. Just in the last couple of days the dandelions have blossomed. The lawn around the house is dotted with their fierce yellow. Most people call them weeds, but my grandmother taught me to think of them as just another wildflower, one of the earliest of the yellows and the brightest. To be sure, they're best seen from several feet away because their leaves and stems are homely, but they're just right from where I'm standing now. I must have a thousand in my view.

Ben crosses to the barn, where I store the screens and too much else, brings screens back to the house one or two at a time. They're the heavy, old-fashioned sort, wood frames that fit over the windows, six screws apiece. My grandfather made them. You have to remove the screws from the storm windows, then screw the screen frames into the same holes. I keep saying I'll buy modern ones that you just slide the glass up, pull the screen down, but they're tinny and expensive, and the old ones still perform well enough.

I unroll the garden hose and spray cobwebs and lint off the screens, check for rips or holes so gaping they require new mesh. Little holes I just cover with a piece of duct tape on each side. Ben carries the extension ladder and sets it up against the back of the house.

He puts his hand on my shoulder. "Let me be the one who goes up the ladder this year. You stay down below and hold it for me."

"Nonsense," I say. "I've done this all my life."

"But your knees."

Oh, yes, my knees. I yield partway. "You can do the big windows. I'll do the smaller ones."

Ben climbs the ladder. As he brings down each storm window, carries up each screen, I press one shoe against the foot of the ladder. He really doesn't need me standing here—the ladder's plenty stable—but he always did it for me in the past. It's part of our ritual.

He's quieter than usual today. I hope he's not still brooding about Ellen.

We switch places when we're ready for the bathroom windows. I climb the ladder and remove the screws that hold in the old storm. He steadies the ladder. My hand trembles as I work, but the screws come out easily. After all these years, the threads are shot. Ben climbs up a couple of rungs and grips the frame from below as I remove the final screw. Then I lower it down to him.

"See," I say. "I'm doing fine."

"Just be careful."

The last window is mine. I climb up again. As I extract the last screw, I look down and see that Ben's not holding the frame from below. The frame tips forward and falls, sunlight flashing off the glass as it passes. It hits Ben on the way down. I cannot see him, but I hear a thud and a scream—Ben's girly yelp—followed by the crash of the frame on the ground and the shattering of glass. I clutch the ladder with both hands, spots pulsing in front of my eyes. When the spots clear, Ben is walking around swinging his arms over his head.

"Holy shit," he says.

"Are you okay?" I say.

"It hit my shoulder."

"Where were you? You were supposed to climb up and hold onto the frame."

"Me? You were supposed to tell me when you were taking out the last screw. I wasn't even on the ladder when you let go."

"I did tell you."

I think I told him.

"You didn't say a damn thing."

I see blood on his arm and descend the ladder. "Are you all right?"

"Didn't you say last year that you'd buy new windows?"

"I don't recall."

"I swear. This is the last time I'm putting in the old ones."

He's still bleeding. "Let me have a look," I say.

He walks away from me. "It's just a scratch. I'm all right."

"Then hand me the last screen and I'll put it in."

He picks up the screen, but holds it away from me. "You are not going back up on that ladder."

"Give me that screen," I say, trying to grab it out of his hands.

"No," he says, his voice rising. He holds the screen over his head, like a parent teasing a child who wants a cookie. It makes me furious.

"Give me the screen, Ben."

"No."

"Give me the screen, you pansy."

"Pansy! No, I am not giving you the screen, you senile old goat."

I start to laugh. What else is there to do? I sit on the porch step, laughing, struggling to catch my breath. Here we are, behaving like two adolescents. I look up, expecting to find Ben laughing, too. But he's not. He just stands there glaring.

I'm heaving. "I was just joking."

"Sure."

"You called me a senile old fart."

"Not a senile old fart, a senile old goat. After you called me a pansy."

"Then we're even."

"No, we're not even. Not at all. We're not even, because what I said about you was true."

He has very little sense of humor.

He climbs the ladder with the last screen, puts in the screws one by one. The bleeding on his arm seems to have stopped.

"Go in and wash up," I say. "I'll pick up the glass."

"Don't. I'll pick it up later." He heads toward the house.

"Okay," I say, changing tactics. "We'll both take a break. It's almost time for lunch."

"You go ahead and eat. I'm going for a walk." He opens the door for Roscoe. "We'll be back in a while. Come on, Roscoe."

They cross the orchard or what used to be the orchard, now just a dozen gnarled trees, Macouns, Cortlands and Wolf Rivers, that I no longer spray. They bear fruit, but only Roscoe eats them, Roscoe and the worms and the deer. Ben and Roscoe disappear into the woods.

I fetch a bucket and gardening gloves from the tool shed, begin picking up the shattered glass. I can't let Roscoe into this part of the yard until it's clear. Fortunately, much of the glass still hangs within the frame, and most of the pieces on the ground are large, easy to find. But when the sun comes from behind a cloud, I see the sparkle of fragments everywhere, most too small for me to see up close, but large enough, I fear, to slice a paw.

Eventually, Ben and Roscoe return from their walk. Ben's calmer now. Not talkative but not pouting. We rake up as much of the glass as we can and go inside for lunch. Roscoe, exhausted, flops down on his pad near the wood stove. I slice cheddar cheese and make grilled cheese sandwiches. Ben washes lettuce, slices a cucumber.

"I'm sorry for what I said," he says, as we sit to eat.

"And I'm sorry, too. It was wrong of me to call you what I did."

"But deep down that's you think, isn't it? That I'm a pansy. You still feel ashamed."

"No," I said. "Not shame."

"Then why have you never told Ellen?"

"It isn't shame exactly."

"What would you call it, exactly?"

"I don't call it anything. That's the point. I thought you and I had an understanding that this was a subject better not talked about."

"I don't think we've ever talked about not talking about it," he says.

"That's what I mean. That's the understanding."

"I see," he says. He looks over toward the stove. "For god's sake, Dad, you left the burner on. It's still on under the frying pan." He gets up and turns it off. "Does that happen often?"

"I'd have noticed before anything happened."

"You could burn the house down."

He finishes his sandwich in silence and starts to

clean up. "You know, I don't really care whether Ellen knows. I hardly ever see her. We exchange cards at Christmas. That's about it. So, for the time being, I've decided I won't say anything."

"Thank you," I say. "I appreciate it." He's looking at me, but I'm not looking back. I rinse off my dishes, offer a gift to him in exchange. "I'll call the storm window people early next week."

In mid-afternoon, Ben leaves for Connecticut. I've been waiting for him to go. I take the screwdriver out of the toolbox and head outside. He's left the extension ladder up against the house, because he's coming back soon to clean the gutters. I test the ladder. It's stable. I climb, steadying myself after each step, and remove the screws holding in the last screen Ben installed. Grasping it tightly in one hand, I descend the ladder. I lean it against the house where Ben put it when he brought it from the barn. Then I let a decent interval elapse, pick it up again, climb the ladder and screw in each of the screws, giving an extra twist at the end to make sure each is secure. It was my screen to do.

Black-Eyed Susans

She likes me, but she squints every morning when I come through the screen door, looks wary, suspicious even, though I now know it's because the sun's to my back and she cannot see who it is. She's also nearsighted, wears glasses sometimes, which is unfortunate because she's so pretty without them. She looks too young to be a grandmother.

"Morning, Tom," she says, smiling, pulling a wisp of hair behind her ear.

"Morning, Claudia."

She hands me a stack of newspapers from behind the counter.

"What's all this?" I ask.

"I saved them for you while you were away."

"Oh yes."

"Welcome back."

I pour myself a cup of coffee from the self-service stand, add a little milk. "I'll sit on your porch and read them."

Roscoe, freed from the car, lies at my feet as I leaf through several issues of the *Valley News*. Skimming five days' papers in one sitting has much to recommend it: I can still remember Monday's stories when reading Wednesday's paper. Early in the week, a truck rear-ended Mildred Rogers as she turned left into the Grand Union. They rushed her to the hospital. In the next day's paper, she's reported in stable condition. By the end of the week, she's home, beginning to walk.

I could have been in the papers myself this week, a human-interest story about a broken-down old man who travels to Connecticut alone, by train, to visit his son. A couple of days later, yielding to pressure, he makes a deposit of one thousand dollars on an apartment in a home for the aged where he swore he'd never live. The day after that, he takes the train home to start packing up his life.

Claudia joins me on the porch with a mug of coffee. "Saturdays it's the regulars plus the tourists," she says, settling herself into the neighboring rocker. Her daughter Lacey and Lacey's husband Andy own the store. Claudia lives with them and their kids in the apartment upstairs.

"You look tired," I say, noticing the shadows under her eyes. Usually she wears silver jewelry from the Southwest, American Indian stuff. Dangly earrings, jangly bracelets. No jewelry at all this morning.

"I've barely slept since the baby came home from the hospital."

Lacey must have had her baby. She's been pregnant.

"Zach was six weeks early, you know. Poor little

thing, not quite five pounds."

Now I remember.

"And he's colicky. So I'm working downstairs while Lacey's taking care of Zach and, of course, Penny and Katie, too. The girls have moved into my room because Lacey needed their room for the baby, and I'm sleeping on the fold-out in the living room." She takes a sip of coffee, returns to talking. She is a talker. "Lacey always said she was going to stop after two, and I came to believe her since Katie's starting first grade in September. But then last fall she and Andy go off for a week by themselves, leaving me with the girls, and come back pregnant. That's the thanks I get for giving them a vacation."

I think she expects me to laugh, so I do, but I've been listening more to her silky voice than her words. Comfort food.

"Anyway, Zach's healthy," she adds.

"It must be crowded up there," I say, "all of you on one floor."

"Crowded? Oh my Lord. I can't even open the couch out into a bed until Lacey and Andy turn in."

Her arm idles over the side of the chair, ruffling Roscoe's back. He rolls over, luxuriating as she tickles his stomach, one of his back legs scratching the air in time with her fingers. I look over at her face. She's silhouetted against the gas pump at the front of the store. I wish it were my stomach she was scratching.

And that's when it comes to me, in a flash of inspiration.

"Why don't you come live with me?" I say.

She laughs. "Do you have something better to offer than a hide-a-bed?"

"I'm serious, Claudia."

She's taken aback. She lifts her hand from Roscoe and turns toward me, uncertain how to react. She keeps smiling, but with a quizzical expression, prepared for me to be joking. "Why, Tom," she says, winking, "are you proposing?"

"I don't think so."

"What are you doing?"

I try to control my excitement. "I'm thinking. You live in this small apartment with five other people and not enough room. I live alone, in a large house, with bedrooms to spare."

"Why, you are serious."

Suddenly it's not just chit-chat anymore. The more I'm thinking the more serious I become. "I'm just two miles from the store, a little less, actually."

"On Schoolhouse Road."

"Yes."

"Lacey's pointed it out."

I don't want to seem too enthusiastic. It might scare her off. "Think about it," I say.

"I should think about it," she says, not looking at me, looking up at the porch roof. Lacey is probably right above her, pacing with the baby. "I never planned to be here this long. I came four years ago, right after I left Lacey's father, which I should have done twenty years before, but anyway I came because Andy and Lacey had just bought the store and needed help with the girls. It turned out I was useful in the store" — I nod — "and I just never got around to returning to Albany."

"Albany? I thought you came from Arizona."

"That's what most everyone thinks. That or Texas. But, no, it was Albany. I always felt dowdy in Albany. I began to dress this way after I started going to square dances, which is where I met Lacey's dad. That's also when I started calling myself Claudia instead of my real name, which was Clara. I hated Clara. It sounded so cow-like."

"I was married once," I say. "And, would you believe, her name was Claudia, too."

"Oh, dear," she says, laughing. "Maybe I better change back to Clara."

"No, Claudia's a beautiful name."

There's a slightly awkward pause.

"Anyway," she says, "when Lacey got pregnant again, I knew I'd have to move, but then Zach came early and I've been so busy I haven't had a moment to think. But I should think, think about your offer. I really should. It's very kind of you."

"You don't have to decide today," I say, wanting her to agree right now.

"Do you know what sort of rent you'd be asking?"

"Rent? I haven't thought about it. No, I don't think there would be any rent."

Her brow furrows. "Exactly what sort of relationship are you looking for, Tom?"

Exactly what sort of relationship does she think

I'm capable of?

"I'll tell you the truth, Claudia. I've reached the point where I could use some help."

"Really? But you look so fit."

"Oh, I am fit for someone eighty-two. Still, it would be a help to have someone else at the house. Ben worries about me. I'm getting forgetful. And he's afraid I might fall and not be able to get to the phone. You being there would give him peace of mind."

She nods.

"He had me down in Connecticut the last few days looking at one of these senior homes."

"Ah, that's where you were. And what did you think?"

"It may be where most folks my age should be, but I didn't care for it. Too many people too close together."

"And would they let you keep Roscoe?"

"They said he could live with me, but whenever we went outside he would have to be on a leash."

Claudia resumes scratching Roscoe's stomach. "And you and he would rather live here, of course."

I feel tears coming to my eyes. "You could move in next week, if you like," I say, then realize that once again I'm moving too fast. "Or whenever you like."

She rocks for a moment, looks up at the ceiling again. "You're quite serious?"

"Absolutely."

"Then, yes, I'd like to come over and take a look."

Roscoe and I return home, me whistling, and I'm shocked when I open the kitchen door. I come in and out ten times a day but never notice what a wreck it is. It's not that it's messy. I put things away when I'm done with them, and for the past few years, a young woman — Axel Grimmer's youngest daughter actually — comes in twice a month and scrubs the kitchen and the bathrooms, vacuums up Roscoe's hair. No, the problem is that everything looks shabby. The rugs, the chairs, the cushions, everything is worn and dark, everything brown or green or orange. I bought the new couch and arm-chair when I moved in after my grandmother died, but that was forty years ago. I left her wallpaper in the dining room, because she loved it so. It's silver, with shiny, skinny Chinamen carrying water buckets. Gram thought it looked elegant. But it's aged, of course, and faded unevenly. And it has all these dark stains next to the china cupboard where the pipe burst.

Claudia probably wants to live in a place that's painted white like the rooms at the old peoples' place. That seems to be the fashion these days. Ben and Morris said it looked cheery. Cheery, my foot. It made me snow blind.

Claudia's coming in just a few hours, and here's my exercise bicycle right in front of the TV. What will she think of that?

I try to drag the bike away, but the stand digs into the carpet. I'd forgotten how much the damn thing weighs. I bend my knees and hoist one end, swivel it a few inches, go to the other end and swivel it a few inches the same direction, eventually get it close to the wall. I'm sweating, heaving, feel a twinge in my back, pain in my legs. This is crazy. Either she likes the house or she doesn't.

I hope she likes it.

Roscoe and I climb upstairs. I open the doors into the two extra bedrooms, open the windows, fluff up the pillows. To remind me after my nap, I take a piece of paper and write "Claudia's Coming" in large letters, tape it to the mirror in the bathroom next to the note that says "FLOSS!"

She's coming after she finishes work.

At lunchtime, Roscoe and I eat on the back porch. It's full summer now. Black-fly season's over. The leaves on the maples and the ashes and the poplars are deep greens, the meadow dotted with wildflowers. I should bring some flowers into the house to add some color. They're mostly yellow at this time of year. Buttercups and cinquefoil and hawkweed and butter-and-eggs and the what-do-you-call them, the ones with tassels. All of them some shade of yellow. And the black-eyed Susans have just begun to bloom. I'll pick some of those.

I retrieve a bucket and the gardening scissors from the tool shed, and work my way across the near hillside snipping flowers. Roscoe shuffles behind. In the pantry, I unearth some dusty vases that belonged to my mother, but only one seems right. It's clear glass, not too frilly. I fill it and place it in the center of the dining room table. I put the rest of the flowers into drinking glasses and take them into the living room.

The phone rings. It's Claudia. "How about if I come over now?" she says.

"Now?" I say, looking at my watch, trying not to sound too eager. "That would be fine."

"It's earlier than I said, but I've got a free hour."

I won't get a nap before she arrives, but I'm too excited to sleep. She's going to say yes. That's what I'm feeling.

I inspect the downstairs again. Suddenly the black-eyed Susans look all wrong: silk purses in a house full of sows' ears. She'll figure out right away that I cut them just for her. Then she really will think I plan to seduce her. I was going to put on a clean sport shirt before she came, shine my shoes, but I think I'd better stay as I am.

I pick up Mother's vase and the four glasses and stash them in the coat closet. I don't throw the flowers out. They cheer the place up. I'll bring them back out after she leaves.

Roscoe barks when Claudia pulls into the driveway. She's changed clothes. I don't remember what she was wearing this morning, but it wasn't this blue dress. And she's put on silver bracelets and a turquoise necklace. She's not really dressed up. She's wearing sandals. But I think she wants to make a good impression. That's a good sign. Roscoe's tail is wagging as it does for no one but Ben and me. He must figure he's going to get his stomach scratched.

"What a fine old house," she says, as she climbs

the front steps. "I've always admired it from the road. Your family's lived here a long time?"

"More than a hundred years," I say. "My great-grandfather built the house himself." It's actually close to a hundred forty, but I don't want to sound boastful.

She steps inside. In the dining room and living room, I wait for her to remark on the wallpaper or the family dining table, but she just smiles at everything. "It's all so relaxed," she says. "It makes you want to take off your shoes and put your feet up."

I think she likes it.

She peers closely at the shelf of family photographs, especially at a picture of my parents and my brother and sister and me when I was in grade school, another of me in my Navy uniform.

"That's you?" she asks.

I nod.

"A girl in every port, I'll bet."

She smiles. I blush.

"My father was in the Navy," she says. "I was born on the day the Japanese surrendered. He was overseas."

I try to calculate how old that makes her. Sixty something. Sixty-one. "That was a couple of years after I enlisted," I say. "Shortly after high school."

She looks closely at another photograph, but I think she's computing how old I am. The answer is I'm old enough to be her father.

She follows me up the stairs. I hold the railing, but lightly, try not to pant, feel a bit dizzy at the top. It's not just the climb. I've also been holding my stomach in, trying to look trim.

"You could have this room," I say, showing her the smaller bedroom first. Her hands look so soft. The room has only a single bed and one window, but she might prefer it since it would give her more privacy. "Or you could have this one." And I show her the larger room, which backs up to mine but which has windows on two sides and a view up the hill.

I don't take her into my bedroom, because she might misinterpret my motives, but we do look into the bathroom, and she walks straight over to the old tub.

"What do you think?" I ask.

"Fit for a queen," she says, patting the porcelain.

And she's right. It's claw-footed, ponderous, long enough to stretch out in. I don't use it anymore because I might slip getting in or out. I use the shower stall my grandparents added sometime in the fifties. But now I'm picturing Claudia helping me into the tub, sponging my back.

She smiles when she sees the note over the sink. "Claudia's Coming," she reads aloud. "Now that's an excellent idea."

I follow her down the stairs, admiring the confident way she carries her shoulders, hoping she doesn't notice that I'm relying on the railing. I pour water for us—I should have made iced tea before she came—and we sit together out back, on the porch.

She puts her hands on her knees and leans toward me. "If you're still serious about the offer, I think I'd like to accept."

"Oh, I'm extremely serious," I say.

"At least on a trial basis. For a few months. We'll see if it works for each of us."

"A trial basis," I echo. "That would be fine." I'd rather it be forever. Still, this is so much better than I dreamed possible. I look at her. I can hardly believe my luck.

"If it's all right with you, I think I'd prefer the second bedroom, the bigger one."

"It may need a new mattress," I say. "I'd be glad to buy a new mattress."

"I was just worried that if I take that room, Ben will find it difficult to visit."

"He can use the small room."

"But how about his partner?"

I didn't know she knew about Morris. She must have met him at the store. "What about him?"

"There's only a twin bed."

I hadn't thought about that. "I'll worry about it when the time comes."

We sit in silence for a moment.

"I like the airiness of the bigger room," she says, "the way it faces this direction onto the hillside. Just look at all these flowers. Even black-eyed Susans. They must be the first of the year. They're my favorites."

"Excuse me a minute," I say. I pull myself up and go inside to the closet, bringing out the vase full of flowers. "These are for you."

She smiles. "Really? They're gorgeous."

"The vase is for you, too."

"Oh my goodness."

"It belonged to my mother."

"Well then you shouldn't just give it away."

"No, no. It's for you."

"Are you sure? Well, thank you. Thank you very much. That's so generous." She's still smiling. I imagine taking her hand, stepping off into the yard, ambling through the meadow. I have a spring in my step. We lie in the grass, her head on my stomach, my hand in her hair.

"I've already been hearing today about how generous you are," she says.

"Beg pardon?"

"Ellie Potter was in the store early this afternoon."

"Yes?"

"She's Dick Potter's mother. She told me about Dick and Debby's house and the mistake they made in the building and what you did for them."

"Oh, that."

"I almost cried when she told me. It made me pretty certain I'd accept your invitation. That and seeing how pretty everything is here. This lovely old house, the trees, the field, the flowers. I've always imagined living in a place like this."

I look at her closely. She's nodding at me, smiling. But it's not a smile of friendship. Suddenly I see her for what she is, for what she really is. I should have known. How could I have been so blind? She wants my house, my trees, my fields, flowers, everything. She thinks I'm an easy mark.

"Are you all right?" she asks.

"I'm fine," I say, faking a smile.

I remember reading about this rich Texan, even older than I am. He fell in love with a girl after seeing her naked in *Playboy* magazine. She got him to marry her and then he died and she inherited all his money.

"Actually, I'm not fine. My stomach hurts."

"You don't look well. Can I get you something?"

"I should probably lie down."

She stands and offers me her arm.

"I can do it myself," I say, forcing myself up.

She follows me inside. I lie on the sofa. She brings me a pillow from the armchair, and I catch her scanning the room again. Sizing it up. She sees me watching.

"I'm looking for another pillow," she says.

Likely story.

She peers at me closely. "You look like you're worried."

That takes me by surprise. I should right away say, no, it's just my stomach, but suddenly she reminds me of Claudia, the other Claudia, my wife Claudia, who could always tell what I was thinking, which was another reason I left.

"I'll bet you're worried about sharing the house with someone else," she says.

Yes, worried about sharing the house with someone who'll rob me blind. "Yes, a little."

"I understand. That's why I proposed a trial basis."

I remain on the couch, even though I suspect she knows I don't have a stomach ache.

"Would you like some tea? I could make some for you."

"No, I'll be all right. I think maybe I'll take a short nap."

"If you're sure I can't do anything, I'll be going," she says. She picks up the vase of flowers and leaves it in the middle of the dining room table. "They look beautiful here, don't they?" From the doorway, she gives me a concerned look. "We both need to think this over. It might not be right for either of us."

Our eyes meet just before she closes the door. I know immediately what I should have known all along. Hers aren't the eyes of a gold-digger. What was I thinking?

I'm embarrassed. I want to get up and call after her, but what would I say?

I pull myself up from the couch and pour a glass of water. I don't want her to change her mind, but she probably will. I'll bet I remind her of her former husband. I suspect I remind a lot of women of their former husbands. I've just shown her I'm temperamental, unsteady, a little creepy even. Who'd want to live with that?

"Roscoe," I say.

His tail wags.

"Would you like to take a walk? Come on, big

fellow." I open the back door. He lumbers down the steps from the porch to the yard. "Roscoe, you're my friend. You never make me act stupid."

The Shower

Deafening pain in my groin, in my hip. A solar flare. Boiling oil. Over my thigh, into my gut.

And water too. Torrents of water, sizzling, steaming. I howl. An animal roars inside my head.

I faint again, I think. And when I come to, the pain is fire but the water has turned to ice. Everything still white.

Between waves, I see where I am. I'm in the shower, folded at the bottom, fetally folded, on my side. I can tell it's the shower because the drain's a few inches from my nose. Why I am here I do not know. I never lie down in the shower.

Somewhere above me are the faucets. I lift an arm to turn them, but pain shoots me in the leg, in the balls. Something must be broken, my hip or my back, something. I scream again, but nothing comes out. It doesn't matter. No one's at home. I push my head back and the shower door swings open. Roscoe stands whimpering on the other side. I seem to be lying on the pain itself. I wriggle forward, pulling with my free hand. Screaming helps even without sound, keeps me from noticing the pain as I edge over the lip of the stall.

I curl my knees as much as I can to get beyond the icy water. My head's against the toilet. I lie shaking until the sun begins to warm me through the window glass. As I shiver less, the pain gets worse.

I use my elbow to turn from my side to my back, find that I can scream out loud.

If Roscoe were smarter, if he were like Lassie, he would race down the stairs, leap through a window and rouse a neighbor. But he just curls up next to me, while I stare at the underside of the toilet.

If I lie perfectly still, I do not need to squeeze my fist against the pain. I'm faint and exhausted, but I must not rest. I must get to the telephone. Perhaps I can scoot out of the bathroom on my back, scoot into the bedroom a few inches at a time, reach the phone on the bedside table. I use one leg, one foot, push tentatively into the floor, into the pain, turn myself very slowly toward the door, push some more. Backstroking.

"Stop it, Roscoe," I say. He's licking my thigh. He senses where it hurts most.

The bathroom door is closed. I usually leave it ajar, because it sticks in summer. I raise my arm toward the handle, but more pain pummels me when I twist the knob. It turns, but I cannot hold the turned knob and pull the door open at the same time. My hand drops to my side. I will lie here a while, build energy, give the door another try.

I have to remember to fix that door.

The phone rings. It's probably Ben. He's the only

one who calls this early in the morning. Maybe he'll be worried when I don't answer. Maybe he'll call the police. But, no, he won't worry. He'll assume I'm outside with Roscoe. "Answer the phone, Roscoe," I say.

What I need to do right now is pee. I should have peed while I was lying on my side. Now I'll have to pee on myself, if I can make myself pee at all in this position. I'm not feeling the need to poop. I should be all right for a while in that department. These days I sometimes go three days without a poop.

I swivel my head and look around the room. I cannot reach my towel. It's draped over the shower stall. The only thing within reach is the wastebasket. I tip it over, pick stuff off the floor a bit at a time and hold it to my face. Nothing but snotty Kleenexes, an empty toothpaste tube. What did I expect?

Above the sink, I see two notes taped to the mirror. I can make out the first one. It says "FLOSS!" I lift my head and squint, but cannot quite decipher the second. I see a capital "C." Two capital C's. "Claudia" something. "Claudia's Coming." That's what it says. "Claudia's Coming." Oh, my god.

Claudia. I haven't seen her in twenty-some years, not since Ben's graduation from college. Why is she coming? Why would she be coming here?

Maybe she's already here.

"Claudia," I squeak, then stop. I don't want her seeing me like this. If I have to face her, I want to do it clothed. Clothed and standing up.

I use my good foot to approach the door from a slightly different angle and reach up once again. With one hand, I grip the knob and turn, ignoring the pain, but the door won't budge.

I'll probably die here. I'll starve to death. I'll die of dehydration. Roscoe and me both. This is the way I'll be remembered: his skeleton lay on the bathroom floor with the shower still running. People always remember an embarrassing death.

I never cashed those bonds. I never put a new roof on the barn.

I never thanked Ben.

Roscoe lifts a leg and pees against the bathtub. The pee flows my way.

I lie very still, eyes closed. After a while, I feel woozy, drowsy.

I'm roused by Roscoe barking. My reflex is to try to sit up. I rise a few inches, scream. Roscoe is standing right by me at the closed door. Maybe he hears someone. Yes, yes, I do, too. I hear knocking at the front door. Hallelujah.

"Hello," I shout, feebly. "We're up here."

The knocking stops. A minute later I hear it again, from a different direction. Whoever it is must have gone around to the back door. It might be Ben. He's the one who visits. "Ben."

No, it wouldn't be Ben. He'd just walk in. The door isn't locked.

I hear a car back out of the driveway. "Don't go," I whisper.

Marooned on a desert island, I wave my shirt but

the ship sails by.

It might have been Claudia who knocked. I think I recall her knock.

I hear a car pass slowly by, pray that it will turn into the driveway. It doesn't. Another car passes. It doesn't stop. It doesn't even slow down.

Perhaps I can use the towel bar on the back of the door and pull myself into a sitting position. It should be possible. I grip the bar with one hand and raise my shoulders a few inches off the ground. I tighten my stomach muscles to try to rise and pain radiates from my thigh up into my arms, into my head. I rise a few more inches and black out, collapse to the floor. A few minutes later, I try again, get even less far.

Ordinary people perform feats of great strength during a crisis. Lift a refrigerator. Shove their way through bolted doors. I cannot even sit up. What is the matter with me?

I stare at the ceiling listening to the shower. Roscoe, whimpering, rests his head on my arm.

Will whoever was at the door please come back? You tried both the front and back doors. That probably means you heard Roscoe barking inside and know that Roscoe and I are almost always together. And if I was inside with him, but didn't come to the door, you'd think that I'm probably in trouble. Or would think, if you knew me well enough.

Unfortunately, only Ben knows me that well. Ben and Claudia, I suppose. She knew me better than anyone. But she wouldn't know me now, would she? Forty years later. Wouldn't know what to make of the car in the driveway, wouldn't know what Roscoe's bark means.

I just peed on myself.

If that was Claudia, perhaps she'll come back. She'll call Ben and he'll tell her the doors are unlocked. She'll come upstairs, find me on the floor, rescue me.

Rescue me? Yes, she'd rescue me, but before she did, she'd peer down at me, see me naked, damaged, defenseless. "Richly deserved," she'd say. And then she'd recite all the ways I annoyed her. The lists I made for her of things to do. My indifference to her clothes. She'd say I was a know-it-all and a cheapskate. She'd say I was sullen. Suspicious. Sarcastic. She'd say, You didn't like my friends. You didn't like my children. You never tried to understand me.

Roscoe is panting, looking at me for answers, looking at me to save him.

"I'm doing the best I can," I say to him. "I've done the best I could."

The bathroom's an oven now with the window closed and the door shut and the morning sun beating down. I feel pain whenever I move even a millimeter, whenever I breathe. I'm bathed in sweat.

Suddenly Roscoe begins to bark again, stands up and barks.

"Tom," someone shouts from downstairs. From the kitchen, I think. It's a woman's voice. "Tom," she says again. It doesn't really sound like Claudia, but then who knows what she'd sound like after all these years?

"Tom, where are you?" Whoever it is is at the bottom of the stairs.

"Tom, are you here? It's me, Claudia."

It is Claudia! Oh my god.

"Shh, Roscoe," I whisper. "Stay very, very quiet."

Possibilities

The toothy lady at the reception desk lends me a note pad and a pen. I put them into the basket that hangs from my walker and clomp, six-footed, to the terrace, lower myself onto the padded bench that overlooks an overplanted garden. I'm in a rehabilitation center forty minutes from home. It's preferable to the hospital but not by much. I can wear my own clothes. No buzzers go off in the hallway in the middle of the night. I'm free to sit outside. Still, I hate the regimentation, hate the air-conditioning, hate being a cripple.

Stony Hill called Ben last week and said my name had risen to the top of their waiting list. They have an apartment available now — now, as in right now. They thought I'd be pleased.

I smooth the notepad on my lap. At the top of the first sheet I write "Something Other Than Stony Hill" in capital letters. Below it I write "Options," underline it twice, lick the pen tip (an old, unhealthy habit), underline "Options" again. I'm hoping if I put all the possibilities down on paper I'll feel less anxious.

I write:

"1. live at home with Claudia and Roscoe."

Sadly, ceremoniously, I draw a line through it.

"2. live at home with Roscoe.

"3. live at Ben's house in CT."

I try to think of more, but nothing comes to mind.

That's about it, I guess.

"4. Die."

Dazzling Claudia has broken my heart. She saved my life and broke my heart. She'd agreed to move in with me, agreed, to be more precise, to move into the bedroom next to mine. But she's changed her mind. She visited the hospital wearing the turquoise necklace and carrying black-eyed Susans she'd picked on my hillside. My heart swelled. She handed me a bag and inside were two tomatoes from the garden — Early Girls, the first of the season. My heart swelled some more. And then she said, "Tom, I've thought hard about it, and it just won't work. You'll need someone with you all the time now and I still have my job at the store." I protested. "I won't need someone all the time." She shook her head. "I just don't want the responsibility." "Claudia, marry me," I said. She just chuckled. "Now stop it, Tom. We have to be realistic."

Beware of women, even bearing gifts.

Since she won't live with me, my second choice would be to live at home by myself, just me and Roscoe. I could do it if I wanted to. After all, it is my house, my choice. No one can stop me unless

I'm incompetent or crazy, which I'm not. All I've done is break a few bones, crack a rib, catch a touch of pneumonia. None of those means I'm crazy. In fact, for the last week or so, my mind's been clearer than it's been in months. Ben said so. And I'm over the pneumonia.

My hip and pelvis are the only problems. They've been stuck back together with metal pins. And I've already started walking, improving faster than they expected. I'll probably be discharged early next week. I could insist on going home. I could sleep on the first floor until I'm able to climb stairs. "Roscoe and I might just take our chances," I told Ben last week, but he kept right on talking as if he hadn't heard me.

He knew I was bluffing. Of course I was bluffing. The truth is I'm afraid to live alone. I'm afraid of slipping in the shower again. I'm afraid of dying, unfound, at the bottom of the basement stairs.

Still, wouldn't I rather die in my own cellar than have to live at the old peoples' shelter, a place where every apartment is painted refrigerator white, where they serve dinner at the same time every afternoon? The answer is: yes, absolutely. I won't cross it out.

I look back at the note pad: "3. Live at Ben's house in CT."

The last possibility. Not a great one, but I could make do. Ben's house is all on one floor. That's good. There's also a yard for Roscoe and a vegetable garden, excellent doctors nearby in New Haven. The obstacle is this: though Morris and I have come to like each other, I'm not at all sure he and Ben want to share the house with me. There's only one extra bedroom, and Morris uses it as an office.

But hey. Here's a better idea. Instead of me moving to Connecticut, how about Ben quitting his job and moving up here? I've had this idea before, but gave it up when he and Morris started living together. But why don't they both come? Of course. I should have thought of this before. They could sleep upstairs, in my room even. My bed would come downstairs. Ben could find a high-paying position in Hanover. Morris—I cannot recall what sort of work Morris does—but he does it from home and up here he wouldn't have to work at all. They'd save so much money living with me that Morris and I could take care of the house and tend the garden together. Morris knows as much about gardening as I do. We'd grow enough vegetables to feed the three of us all summer. We could freeze some, can some, pickle some. That would save even more.

At the top of the sheet, right under Options, I squeeze, "Live at farm with Ben and Morris." I underline it. I'll tell Ben as soon as he comes. He and Morris are driving up this afternoon. Roscoe will be with them. He's been staying with them since the accident. I tear the sheet from the notepad, tear a second sheet in case I have more ideas, return the pad and pen to the woman at the reception desk, who thanks me in a gooey voice she probably also uses for puppies and babies.

When Dr. Spencer said that he'd arranged for

me to come to a rehabilitation center, I thought he was talking about the kind of place where alcoholics dry out. But the patients here aren't drunks, or at least they aren't here because they're drunks. They're here because they fell or got hit by a car or had a stroke or surgery. I have two physical therapy sessions every day, one in just a few minutes. Bend, Mr. Whitaker. Bend a little further. Now hold it. Hold it a little longer. Very painful. And at the end, the therapist smiles and says "Good work, Mr. Whitaker. Now you have a nice day." I also have to put up with the other patients, who complain about their children, about the rules against smoking, about the food. Me, I never complain, not out loud. I barely talk to the other patients at all.

Ben arrives after lunch, with Roscoe but without Morris. The three of us sit on the terrace because dogs are not permitted inside. Roscoe wiggles his stump of a tail, rubs against my good leg, lies with his head on my foot.

I take my sheet of notes out of the basket on the walker.

"I've had an idea," I say.

"What's that?" says Ben, who sits next to me on a cushioned bench.

"How's your job going these days?" I ask.

"About the same. Fine."

"Still, you'd be happier living up here, wouldn't you? At the farm." That comes out a bit more abruptly than I'd planned, but I plunge ahead. "I think that you and Morris should come live with me at the farm. You could take over the upstairs. You could use one bedroom for sleeping, another as a sitting room."

He crosses one leg over the other, looks forlorn, distracted.

"I'd live downstairs in the study."

"Dad," he says.

"Fortunately, there's already a shower in the downstairs bathroom."

"Dad, we've already talked about this."

"About the shower?"

"Maybe not that particular detail."

"So what do you think?"

"I have a fine job in Connecticut."

A machine starts up somewhere. A woman with her neck in a brace takes a seat in one of the rockers.

"But you love the farm."

"Of course I love the farm. I hope to live there someday when I retire."

"You're too young to retire."

"Exactly."

"You could find an excellent job in Hanover. I'm sure of that."

"I want to stay where I am, Dad."

He's stubborn, self-centered.

A nurse's aide comes onto the terrace, hands me a glass of water and a pill in a paper thimble, leaves without saying a word. She and I have learned how to work with each other.

"I want you to think about it," I say, "and I'd like

to talk it over with Morris."

"No, you will not talk it over with Morris. This is just between you and me."

I fold my arms across my chest, turn my shoulders toward him, even though I feel a zap of pain in my hip. "If I were a homosexual," I say, "would you move up here?"

"What?"

"I think that the reason you don't want to move up here is that you don't want to live with someone like me."

His eyes open wide, as if I'd said something totally irrational. "No, that's not it at all."

"Well, let me ask a slightly different question. If I were homosexual, would you and Morris make room for me to live at *your* house?"

"You're really desperate, aren't you?"

"Well, would you?"

He doesn't answer. I think I've got him.

"Dad, I need to tell you something. Morris and I are separating. Morris is moving out." He purses his lips tightly.

"Morris is leaving you?"

He nods.

"Is it because of me? I've been worrying that he's angry about your coming up here so often."

"No, it's not because of you. It's because of me. He says I'm crotchety and too used to doing things my own way. He says I lived alone for too many years." He pauses, rests a hand on my knee. "It turns out, apparently, that I'm a lot like you."

I'm startled. "Don't talk that way, Ben. You're a much nicer person than I am."

"It's kind of you to say."

"Shame on Morris."

He reaches across and takes my glass of water, sips from it, wipes his eyes on his sleeve. I put a hand on his arm, squeeze gently. He starts crying again and leans his head on my shoulder. He hasn't done that since he was little. I put my arm over his shoulder.

After a short while, he sits up, looks over at the neck-braced woman on the rocker, who is looking back at us. He clears his throat. "Stony Hill called again this morning," he says. "They talked to Dr. Spencer yesterday, and he and they agree that you need a different apartment than the one that's available now. You need one that will offer more assistance."

"I see. More assistance."

"They expect the right sort of unit to be ready in six or eight weeks. In the meantime, I suggest that you come to Connecticut and live with me."

"Come again."

"I propose that when you leave here next week, you and Roscoe come and live with me until the apartment is ready."

The governor calls at the eleventh hour and postpones the execution. "I'd like that very much," I say.

A wave of serenity passes over me, rapidly succeeded by anxiety. "But what about the farm? Who will look after the farm?"

"Claudia says she's willing to live there."

"No. Remember she said she wouldn't."

"She isn't willing to look after you, Dad, but she's willing to live at the house."

"She said that?"

"Yes."

"What a waste. Her there without me."

"Dad, it wouldn't have worked, her taking care of you. You know that."

"It would have worked for me."

"We'll stop at the farm on the way to Connecticut. You can pick up the clothes and other stuff you'll want while you're staying at my house."

"Perhaps I can help patch things up between you and Morris."

He makes a sad little snort and looks off toward the gardens. I pull myself up with his help, and he and I loop slowly around the terrace with its ugly but reassuring rubberized surface. Roscoe tags along behind, almost as stiff as I am. He's slowing down.

"One thing," Ben says, "for at least a couple of weeks, we'll need to arrange for a home health worker. I think your insurance will cover up to six months."

"Six months at your house would be fine," I say.

"It won't be anywhere near that long. Another apartment will be available well before then."

"Six months with you would be fine, even a year."

"You old rogue," he says. "You weasely old rogue. After a year we'd both be crazy."

Teresa

It's mid-afternoon and I'm carrying beets from Ben's garden to the old couple who live two doors down from him. Yesterday I carried beets to the widow who lives two doors down on the other side. I feel slightly hypocritical. I hate beets. I volunteered to deliver them because it's good exercise for my hip and because it lets me get away from Mrs. Sigoures, a tyrant, a shrew, a home health aide.

I reach the old couple's front steps and the lady opens the door smiling as if she already knows me.

"Hello," I say. "I'm Tom Whitaker, Ben's father."

"I thought that's who you were. I've seen you pass along the road."

I'll bet she's one of these women who monitors everything that happens in her neighborhood. And out here, it's probably a major event when anyone walks by. Her house and Ben's sit on a road that isn't the fastest way to anywhere. No sidewalks, narrow shoulders. Across the road the white fence of a horse farm stretches more than half a mile. On this side runs a short string of nearly identical ranch houses.

"Come on in. Where is your nice old dog? You're always with your dog. You bring him the next time, you hear?"

Roscoe wanted to come, of course, but I couldn't manage him and my cane and the beets.

"I'm Ruby Brancati," she says, "and this is my husband Pete, and this is Pete's daughter Teresa."

A tall, paunchy fellow and a woman who looks to be in her fifties rise from the sofa.

"One more time," I say, concentrating.

"I'm Ruby. Pete. Teresa."

Pete, who looks to be a few years younger than I am, grips my hand. "Pleased to meet you," he says in a hefty voice, and I recall Ben telling me Pete's retired from the Army. Teresa also stands. She doesn't shake my hand. She barely nods. She's stocky, black-haired, in a gray bathrobe. Absolutely silent. She reminds me of Stonehenge. Still, her face would be pretty if she smiled. Maybe she's not feeling well.

I'm not looking so good myself, if truth be told. I've lost so much weight my pants bunch up under my belt. My windbreaker hangs loose around my shoulders.

"Have a seat," says Pete, motioning to his place on the couch.

I remove my cap and hand Ruby the sack. "Ben asked me to bring you these."

Ruby peeks inside. "Beets! Well, thank you very much. Thank you so much. That son of yours has been so good to us. All summer long, one vegetable after another." She turns to Teresa. "Mr. Whitaker's son is the one who brings us zucchini and tomatoes and Lord knows what all. I thought growing season was over, but here you are with beets."

Beets, of course, do not merit this much enthusiasm.

Pete sits in a recliner without pushing back and I lower myself onto the couch. Ruby flicks off the television and heads toward the kitchen. "I have coffee on. Do you take cream and sugar?" She's talking across the kitchen counter, a counter identical to the one in Ben's house and the widow's house and every other house on this side of the road, I suppose. "Are you just here for a visit?"

"I'm here for a few weeks until I move to an old folks home."

"An old folks home?" she says. "I didn't think they had old folks homes anymore."

"It's called Stony Hill."

She chuckles. "Now, you're pulling my leg, Mr. Whitaker. Stony Hill is like a resort."

"I don't like resorts."

"You don't like Stony Hill?"

"I'm sure it's right for some people, but I have a perfectly fine house in Vermont where I'd rather be."

Ruby puts her hand to her bosom. "We'd move to Stony Hill in a minute if we could afford it, wouldn't we, Pete?"

She hands me a mug and a slice of cranberry bread, expecting, I think, that I'll say more about Stony Hill, but I have nothing to add on the subject. I take a sip and look for a place to rest the mug, but the coffee table's a jumble of newspapers and the table at the end of the couch is blanketed with china do-dads. Ruby sees me looking and picks up the papers. No one says anything.

"Teresa's just come up from Baltimore," Ruby says after a while.

"Ah, yes" I say.

Teresa sits at the other end of the couch, inexpressive.

"Forced out of the home she'd lived in for twenty years."

"Ruby!" says Teresa, but Ruby keeps talking.

"Well, technically, it wasn't Teresa's house. She worked for this family and managed their house, an enormous old house. And then, just a few weeks ago, they let her go. For no real reason. Can you imagine?"

Teresa flushes. I'm embarrassed for her. I turn my head toward the window. "How unfortunate," is all I can manage.

"What was the name of the man who built the place, Teresa?" Ruby rattles on.

Teresa says nothing.

"Langdell, was that it?" says Ruby.

Teresa sighs. "Lambert. Oliver Lambert."

"The Oliver Lambert?" I say, surprised. "Of the Lambert Trust Company?"

Teresa nods.

"You've heard of him?" says Ruby.

"Oh yes," I say. "The Lambert Trust Company

underwrote some of the great railroads in the nineteenth century."

Teresa cocks her head slightly.

"Did you work for one of Lambert's children?" I ask. Lambert himself's been dead for seventy, eighty years at least.

She answers softly. "The house isn't the Lamberts' anymore. I worked for people named Maynard. You wouldn't have heard of them."

"It's a shame to have to leave a house you lived in so long," I say, but as soon as it comes out, I wish I could take it back. Teresa looks on the verge of tears. "Well, at least you have a fine house here to come home to."

Her eyes meet mine. I can tell she knows I'm fibbing. This isn't that fine a house. It's just a house, an ordinary house. Even Ruby would rather live at Stony Hill.

Ruby pours more coffee. "She oversaw everything for the Maynards, all the other help. The Maynards agreed she did wonderful work. Teresa, honey, go get the photograph of the house. Mr. Whitaker would enjoy seeing it. No, really, go get it."

"You don't need to," I say.

Ruby persists. "You don't mind, Teresa, do you?"

Teresa starts to protest but pulls her bathrobe more tightly around her and walks down the hall, returning with a framed photograph, a very old photograph. She hands it to me.

The house is a huge Victorian, with turrets and upstairs porches and a veranda as wide as a moat.

Handsome but ostentatious is what I'd call it. Just what you'd expect of an old robber baron like Lambert. A family of four stands out front.

Teresa sits next to me on the couch. She takes a deep breath and points to a tall man wearing a top hat. "That's Mr. Lambert," she says. "The picture was taken in 1888, just a few years after the house was built." Lambert appears to be in his fifties. "And that's Mrs. Lambert, Fanny Lambert. She was a Livingston from New York. And those are their daughters. Adele the younger one became a poet. Julia died in a boating accident just before the First World War. If you look closely at the front windows, you can see the letter L woven into the leaded glass. See. There and there and there."

I hold the photo just beyond the end of my nose. "I do see it. What a handsome house. How many rooms are there?"

"Nineteen. I have more photos of the inside," she says, almost in a whisper. "They're in one of the boxes that should be coming any day now. I'll show them to you when they get here if you'd like to see them."

When I return to Ben's, I hesitate at the top of the driveway. I'd hoped that Mrs. Sigoures would have left by the time I got back, but her car's still here, and Ben's is here, too. He's home already. It's later than I thought. The door opens and Mrs. Sigoures steps out, buttoning her coat.

"I leave now, Mr. Whitaker. I have talk to your son. He will speak to you." She sidles by me toward her car. She's from Guatemala. She gives me medicines, makes me do my exercises, fixes me lunch.

"Hello, Ben," I say cheerfully, hoping to delay the confrontation I'm sure is coming. "I took the beets to your friends down the road. Very nice people."

Ben hasn't yet changed out of his suit. "We need to talk about Mrs. Sigoures."

"Now?"

"She told me that you kicked her this morning while she was working on your legs."

"It happened by mistake."

"She said she watched you reach your leg back and kick her."

"That is not what happened. And I said I was sorry." I edge past Ben into the kitchen. I wasn't expecting to have to deal with this so soon. I take two glasses out of the cupboard. "Would you like some water?"

"She also said that if something like this happens again, she will not be returning,"

I say nothing.

"What have you got against these people, Dad?"

In truth, I don't quite know what I have against them. I should be trying to please Ben. I don't want to move to Stony Hill. I hand him a glass, which he puts down and ignores, and sit on the sofa, which, by the way, is not nearly as comfortable as the one at the Brancatis'.

"The lady from Puerto Rico didn't last a week. Frankly, I don't know what to do."

"The lady from Puerto Rico peeped at me while I

was in the bathroom, remember."

"She wasn't 'peeping.'"

I wait until he looks me in the eye. "She was outside the house, staring in the window while I sat on the toilet. I call that peeping."

"She looked in because she was concerned."

"I'd told her twice I was all right."

"You were apparently in there a very, very long time."

"I have constipation. Just because I'm constipated doesn't mean I'm not entitled to privacy like anyone else."

Ben squeezes his lips together. "All you need to do is be polite to Mrs. Sigoures. You don't have to like her. The apartment at Stony Hill will probably be ready in a couple more weeks."

"I can barely understand her."

Ben says nothing.

"She's probably in the country illegally. Did you think about that?"

Ben still says nothing.

I rub the back of my hand. "We've been having fun together, you and I."

"When I'm at home, everything's mostly okay. But I cannot stay home all the time."

The next day, after my nap, I dig out a photograph album I brought from home and look through it.

"I'm walking down to the neighbors," I tell Mrs. Sigoures.

"I will walk you," she says. "You put Roscoe on the leash and I carry your book, yes?"

"No thank you," I say. "I'll leave Roscoe here with you."

If she came along, Ruby would invite her in.

Mrs. Sigoures helps me down the front steps. "You be back for your exercises by four, like you promise."

I make my way along the front path and out the driveway. I'm more nicely dressed today, a pullover sweater and a sports jacket with pockets that don't droop.

Ruby steps out the door as I work my way up their driveway. I'd called ahead.

"Nice to see you again," she says.

"I don't have any beets this time."

"Well then you go right back and get some," she laughs. "Come in, come in. I've just taken some macaroons out of the oven."

I sit where I sat the day before. The cushion's warm. Pete must have just gotten up.

He grips my hand again and sits at the other end of the couch. The TV, just turned off, glows slightly. Teresa's nowhere in sight. It hadn't occurred to me that she might not be here.

Ruby seems to sense my disappointment. "Teresa," she calls down the hall, "we have a visitor."

Pete echoes her. "Butterfly, company."

A few minutes later Teresa enters the living room. She looks better today. She's dressed. She's wearing a little lipstick.

I hold up the photo album. "I brought a few photographs I thought you might like. Come sit."

I scoot closer to Pete, patting the cushion beside me. I look up as Teresa sits and think I catch Ruby giving her a wink.

I've placed markers into the album. I turn first to an early page and point to a black-and-white snapshot. "This one's from 1938. It shows the front of the farmhouse. I took it when I was fourteen with a Kodak Brownie my grandparents gave me for my birthday." Ruby leans over Pete's shoulder. "The main part here my great-grandfather built in the 1860s. It's a three-quarter cape. See, two windows on one side of the front door, but only one on the other. A full cape has two windows on each side. He added the rooms on this side later as the family grew. That new room became the kitchen. Everyone's always come in and out the kitchen door."

"And it's been in your family ever since your great-grandfather?" Teresa asks.

"A hundred and forty some years."

"She's going to be jealous," says Pete. "We moved all around while she was growing up. One year here, one year there."

Teresa smirks. "Georgia, Mississippi, Japan, Virginia, Germany, North Carolina, New Jersey, Indiana, Virginia again. So many rundown old bungalows I can't remember which is which, even when I see them in a picture."

I clear my throat and turn to a second photo, at the end of the album. It's the same view of the house, but this one's in color. "I shot this just a couple of years ago, almost seventy years later."

Teresa looks closely. "Nothing's changed much, has it?"

"Only the rocker on the porch."

She nods approvingly. "Good for you for keeping it the way it was."

I also show them a photo of the back of the house and a few of the barn and the hillside. At some point, I notice Ruby peering at a picture of me and Claudia, the first Claudia. I quickly turn to the last marker. "One more," I say. "Here's another fine old building." It's one of those long, two-story structures, red brick with a heavy cornice, that you see in the heart of downtowns all over New England, though this one has nicer details than most. In the center at the top is a wood sign reading "Gifford Block 1882" in gilded letters. I point to the ground level on the left side. "This is the hardware store I ran for many years. I had half the first floor and the entire basement." "Green Mountain Hardware and Supply" reads the awning.

"Is that you?" says Ruby.

I nod. I'm not surprised she isn't sure. I'm standing in front with Clem, a Springer spaniel ancestor of Roscoe's. I had a full head of dark hair then and meat on my bones. I had stature.

"An old family business?" Pete asks.

"No, just me. I worked at a bank down in Concord for many years but never liked it, and when my grandmother died, I moved up to the farm. You couldn't make a living farming by then, so I borrowed and bought the store."

"My, my," says Ruby. "So you owned your own business right downtown."

"Well, it's a small town."

"Still," she says.

I sense that I'm right at the edge of boasting. I feel self-conscious and take a sip of coffee. I look around. "You have so many interesting little statues," I say. The do-dads on the table next to me are not the only ones. Do-dads cover every surface in the room except the coffee table.

"Why thank you," says Ruby.

I'm looking at the mantelpiece, where a bear in a red t-shirt sits with his paw inside a jar.

"That's Pooh," she says. "And next to him is Cinderella. You recognize her, I'm sure." On the base of a small lamp with a frilly shade, a porcelain girl in a baby blue gown dances with a porcelain prince. "And this over here"—we're working our way across the mantelpiece—"is Dumbo."

"Oh," I say. Dumbo is another animal with clothes on. I try to come up with something to say. "For an elephant it has very large ears."

"That's so he can fly," says Ruby.

"You don't say."

"All of them are Walt Disney."

"Well, it's quite a collection." I glance next to me at Teresa. She has her eyes closed. I think she's embarrassed. I feel awkward. "I can't stay long. I promised Ben I'd come home promptly today for my exercises."

"Don't go," says Ruby. "The macaroons should

have cooled enough to eat."

I look over at Teresa again. Her eyes are open, but they're not looking at me. "No," I say, "I really should go."

"Then, Teresa, why don't you walk Tom home?" Ruby suggests.

Teresa doesn't move and Ruby pushes a bit. "You could use the fresh air. You can't stay inside all the time."

"Um, all right," Teresa says. She returns to her room for a sweater, and we leave the house together. Even with a cane I need her help navigating the front steps. She holds my elbow and takes the photograph album.

"I get stiff when I sit too long in one position," I say, steadying myself in the driveway.

"I sit too much myself," she says. She puts her hands into the pockets of the sweater. "I used to get plenty of exercise trooping up and down stairs all day."

"Then let's walk farther."

We pass Ben's driveway without turning in. I hold out an elbow, hoping she'll put her arm through mine, but she misunderstands and cradles my elbow with her hand. I shake my arm slightly and she figures out what I want. We walk arm in arm.

October has many days like this in Connecticut, more even than Vermont. A sky as pure a blue as the year can give. The grass still green if it's been a wet summer. Warm in the sun, cool in the shade, a slight breeze. The leaves beginning to turn, a few beginning to fall. Days you want to hold onto because you know frigid weather is approaching.

We cross to the horse farm on the other side of the road, and a mare trots down the still-lush meadow to the fence. I pull a couple of carrots from my coat pocket. I always carry a few for the horses. "Here, give her one," I say to Teresa.

"I don't know anything about horses," she says. "I'll just watch."

She watches, and when I offer her a carrot again, she follows my example. She doesn't flinch when the mare chomps down almost to her fingers.

"Expertly done," I say.

"I apologize for being so unfriendly yesterday," she says. "It was rude of me. This all just happened week before last."

"I can understand. After twenty-some years."

"The only house I ever lived in long enough to think of as home."

"And then they just let you go."

"Mr. Maynard said it was because the children were grown and had gone off to college. He said they no longer needed live-in help, but I think what was really going on is he just wanted to get rid of me. He and I had issues almost the whole time I worked for them. I hate to say so, but he was a slob. He left cigar butts all around the house. I'd find them in the toilets, in the potted plants, on the edge of the bathtub. He knew it drove me crazy."

"I don't smoke," I say.

"And he had opinions about things he knew

nothing about. I remember in the early years, he and I argued about whether Schuyler was ready to sleep through the night without diapers. What did he know about diapers? Later, after I wasn't just the nanny, we argued about what wax the cleaners should use on the hardwood floors and whether we needed a second vacuum cleaner for the upstairs. And he kept making all these so-called improvements to the house."

She has more spirit in her voice. I think she can tell that I'm really listening.

"At first, I was impressed by it all. Before they even moved in — they moved just a few weeks after I started work for them — he had the wood floor in the library covered with wall-to-wall carpet and had several of the mahogany bookcases taken out and put in a bar, and a television set a yard wide. I was impressed because it cost so much. But after I'd lived there for a while I realized it was a blessing to live in a fine old house that had been kept the same way for a long time. I wish you could see it, all the hand-carved woodwork, the six fireplaces, one of them so big you can almost stand up in it, the high ceilings, the three pantries. I came to like everything the way it was."

I nod.

"A year or so after the move, he took the guest bedroom next to theirs and had it converted it into a gymnasium with a wall of mirrors and marble floors, a rowing machine, and a Jacuzzi. He put in a picture window, too, even though it was totally inappropriate for a Victorian house. Not much later he decided to remove the rose beds that had been in the south garden since the Lamberts, so that he could install a putting green. I told him it would be a shame. Mrs. Maynard actually cried. But he went ahead and did it."

She stops and looks over at me. "I'm talking too much."

"No, not at all."

"You're sure?"

"I'm listening. Go on."

"Anyway, I got so interested in the house I went downtown to the Historical Society, because they had a set of the architect's original plans. The plans were in brown ink, with little notes everywhere. You could see details that were different from the way the house was actually built. Afterwards, I told Mr. and Mrs. Maynard they should go see them. She wanted to, but he didn't even look at me when I was talking about them. He acted as if I were snoopy for even taking an interest."

We walk along the edge of the road. I push myself to maintain a younger man's pace. Three cars pass us, one right after another. This is what counts as rush hour around here. We continue to the end of the horse farm, pausing to look at the fence as it turns and stretches uphill farther than the eye can see. We rest for a few minutes leaning against the fence, then turn back.

As we approach Ben's house, I see Mrs. Sigoures standing at the front window. Teresa notices her, too. "She's a home health aide," I say, wondering why I'm whispering. "I try my best to avoid her."

"She isn't helpful?"

"I suppose she is, but she's pushy like a doctor, even though she isn't even a nurse."

Mrs. Sigoures opens the front door and steps out, looking at her watch. "Mr. Whitaker, I worried about you. You promise you'd be right back."

"Sorry," I say, though I'm sure I don't sound it. I'm looking at Teresa. "Would you like to take another walk tomorrow?"

Teresa doesn't seem to be listening. She's looking at Mrs. Sigoures. Perhaps she's expecting me to introduce her. She nods to Mrs. Sigoures, and Mrs. Sigoures reaches out to help me up the stairs, taking a deep breath of exasperation.

"Would you join me for another walk tomorrow?" I repeat.

Teresa nods. "That would be very nice, Mr. Whitaker. Yes. Thank you for asking."

Mrs. Sigoures leaves at five, which gives me about an hour before Ben comes home, one of the two times a day when Roscoe and I have the house to ourselves. The other is the early morning. I've started getting up before dawn to enjoy the quiet while Ben's still asleep. Roscoe gets up with me, of course. He understands me. He never barks before breakfast. Ben doesn't understand. His alarm is a radio turned up loud so it forces him awake, and then he comes out to the kitchen and turns on another radio while he starts the coffee.

The station he listens to, WPKsomething, is news all day long. Always something unpleasant—an explosion in Iraq, an earthquake in Ecuador, the Nikkei plummeting in Japan. I don't mind reading about these things, but hearing someone else talk about them without any emotion whatever and before breakfast is more than I can take.

Right now, however, it's just Roscoe and me. The dryer was running, but I stopped it. The radio's off. It's almost like being at home. I'm feeling good. Tomorrow Miss Brancati and I will take another walk. I'll tell her more about the farm. I'll hear more about the Lamberts. Spruced up, as she was today, she's a good-looking woman. Deep brown eyes. Good teeth. Ample hips. Maybe we'll come back here after the health lady leaves and have a cup of coffee or even a drink. This is much better than Stony Hill. No one like her lives there, you can be sure of that.

Another Possibility

Wednesday it rained steadily and, though I'd have been willing to brave it, Teresa called and asked to postpone til the next day. Thursday she called again and said she needed to take Ruby to the dentist because Ruby was reluctant to drive after having Novocain. I was beginning to think she was giving me the brush off, but this morning she calls early and invites me to take a walk this afternoon. She sounds as if she really wants to do it.

At exactly two, she arrives at Ben's house.

Mrs. Sigoures fusses at the door. "You should take an umbrella, Mr. Whitaker. They say it's going to rain."

"Nonsense," I say, looking up at the sky.

While Mrs. Sigoures watches out the front window, Teresa and I head off in the opposite direction than we walked before. There's an icy edge to the breeze today. Roscoe bobs behind us on his leash. We move slowly, partly for Roscoe's sake, at a pace that works for conversation.

"Are you warm enough?" she asks.

"I'm fine," I say, though in fact I'm shivering a

little. So little body fat. I should have worn my heavier jacket.

She pulls a scarf from her coat pocket. "Take this. I really don't need it."

"I'm fine," I repeat, but I let her wrap the scarf around my neck.

"I'm actually too warm," she says. "I borrowed this coat from Ruby, and it's got a wool lining. I think it was meant for mid-winter."

"Late fall maybe. You'll need something warmer than that by January,"

"I've never spent a winter in the north. It's even colder up in Vermont, isn't it?"

"Oh, much. We have whole days at a stretch when it doesn't get above zero. What you need to get through a Vermont winter, my grandfather used to say, is four cords of wood and a righteous woman."

She smiles, so I keep on talking and before I know it, I've told her about both my grandparents and about my grandfather's father, who built the house by himself despite a withered leg. She asks good questions that keep me going as we work our way to the far end of the horse-farm fence. When I reach a stopping point, well not a stopping point, but a point to take a pause before my next story, I pull a couple of carrots from my pocket. "I brought some again," I say, "but the horses aren't down at this end of the field today. I suppose we'll have to eat them ourselves."

She doesn't understand that I'm joking so I pretend to gnaw on one of them and she smiles again. She doesn't seem to be the sort of person who smiles just because someone else expects it. I like that. From her coat pocket, she takes a small sack. "I brought something, too" she says. "Date bread Ruby baked this morning. She bakes almost every day to cheer me up."

"Does it help?"

"No, not really, but I eat anyway. I've been eating too much."

"And I don't eat enough. I've shrunk."

"You don't look shrunken to me," she says. "You remind me of Oliver Lambert. You carry yourself the way I imagine he did. Upright. Confident."

She knows how to please.

"Of course, Mr. Maynard was confident, too, but he was confident like a bully." She stops herself. "There I go. I can't stop thinking about him."

"He sounds like a horrible person to work for."

"Yes, nasty right up to the end. Someday I'll tell you about the lamps in the dining room."

"Tell me now."

"No, you were in the midst of talking about your family."

"I'd like to hear."

She pauses, looking reluctant, then starts. "Well, he came down for breakfast one morning—this was just about six weeks ago—and told me they were going to redecorate the dining room. I kept my mouth shut but I thought redecorating was a terrible idea. I think he told me rather than letting

Mrs. Maynard tell me, because he wanted to see my reaction. The dining room was the only room they'd pretty much left alone. The table was the original, sold by the Lamberts' daughter to the next owners and by them to the Maynards. I was afraid Mr. Maynard would replace the oriental rug with the sort of honey beige wall-to-wall carpet he'd put in the library.

"Anyway, when the decorator arrived to meet with Mrs. Maynard, I recalled some bronze wall lamps in a crawl space in the storage room. They had a tag on them that said 'removed from the dining room, 1921.' I brought them downstairs. The decorator took one look and said, 'oh, dear, no, too heavy, too Germanic, too morose,' and I could see Mrs. M didn't much care for them either. She asked me to put them into the back hall with some things she was giving to a resale shop, and I resisted. 'Mrs. Maynard,' I told her, 'the lamps belong with the house.'

"She seemed a bit startled. 'Well, okay, yes,' she said, 'put them back upstairs if you like.' So I returned the lamps to the storage room, but a few days later, I found them in the back hall in the box for the thrift shop. It must have been Mr. Maynard who put them there. He had to have his own way, even though he really didn't care about the lamps one way or the other."

"One last time, I carried them upstairs, but this time I took them to my bedroom and stuck them under my bed. I shouldn't have done that, I know.

They weren't mine. But what else could I do? They'd have been gone forever." She looks at me.

"You had to do it."

"I was afraid Mr. M would notice them missing, so then I did something else I probably shouldn't have. I wrote him a letter saying I'd like to buy the lamps and asking how much he wanted. He never responded. He never said anything about them again. He went out of his way to avoid me for the next week. And ten days later, without any warning, he fired me. I was in the kitchen rinsing my lunch dishes and he walked in and fired me. Just like that. He said that with Jennifer and Schuyler off to college, he and Mrs. Maynard no longer needed live-in help. That was just a lie. With a house that big, of course they needed live-in help.

"He said I could stay while I searched for another job, but that the time had come for me to move on. I remember clutching the edge of the sink to keep from fainting. I don't remember anything else. No, I remember one thing—the sizzle of his cigar, stzzzz, as he dropped it into his coffee mug and left the room."

She stops and holds out a hand. "Do you feel raindrops?"

"What a sad story," I say.

"I think it's starting to rain."

"I'd like to hear the rest," I say.

"That's about it," she says, though I'm sure there must be more.

Neither of us has brought an umbrella. We stand

for a moment gauging the weather, hesitating. Then, as the drops fall more insistently, we turn and head back.

"I'd hoped for a longer walk," I say, resentful that Mrs. Sigoures has been proven right.

"Maybe we can take another tomorrow—if, of course, you'd like to."

"Oh, yes," I say. "And the day after and the day after that."

We trudge, single file, along the edge of the pavement, Roscoe sandwiched between us.

"You're getting wet," I say over my shoulder. "You should go on ahead."

"No, I want to make sure you get back all right."

A thought has been percolating in my head that I cannot keep inside. "You know, I've just had an idea." My voice wobbles a little. We've reached the top of Pete and Ruby's driveway.

"Tell me," she says, ignoring the rain.

"Why don't you come take the health lady's place? I would tell her I don't need her services anymore, and you could come every day instead. I need someone to help me with my medicines and exercises. It would be for just a few weeks until I move into the old peoples' dormitory. Oh, this is good. I'd pay you well."

Teresa's face flushes. "Mr. Whitaker, I am not a home health aide."

"We wouldn't have to call you that," I say.

She looks to be at the edge of tears. "I ran a large house in Baltimore."

I'm confused. "Then I should be easy by comparison."

She looks away from me. I feel pain in my hip, a zing arcing down my leg.

"I thought we were friends," she says, very quietly.

"We are friends. We would have fun together. We can both speak English. We could take walks."

"No," she says, "No thank you, Mr. Whitaker."

"Please call me Tom."

She turns her head and looks toward the house. "Mr. Whitaker, I think I'm ready to go inside."

In late afternoon, I sit in the Danish rocker, the only comfortable piece of furniture in Ben's house, but I'm not relaxed. I upset Teresa. And Ben will be here any minute now and I'll have to talk to him about the health lady. I scan the local paper, which is filled with stories about politicians I've never heard of, high school football games I don't care who won. I turn to the obituaries, with their little photographs, often decades old, of men who enjoyed hunting and golf and women who doted on their grandchildren. Ordinarily, I enjoy reading about people I've outlived, but not today.

Ben pulls into the driveway, and I struggle out of the chair.

"How did your exercises go?" he asks as he carries in grocery bags and a pot of chrysanthemums.

"Okay," I say.

"You don't sound as if they really were okay. Is something wrong?"

"Not really."

"It's Mrs. Sigoures, isn't it? What has happened?"

"She says she's not coming back."

Ben shuts the refrigerator and turns toward me. "Why not?"

"I'm not sure. I've been taking walks the past few days with Teresa Brancati."

"Yes, you told me."

"And when I came back today, I wasn't in any mood to do my exercises. And so Mrs. Sigoures and I had a discussion and at the end of it, she said she wouldn't be coming back."

"What did you say to her?"

"I don't recall."

"Oh, Dad." Ben closes his eyes.

"I made every effort to be polite."

"What are we going to do?" Ben sits on the kitchen stool. "I'll call the agency in the morning, but I won't be surprised if they refuse to send anyone else."

"I don't need anyone else. I can take care of myself. We can set alarm clocks to go off when I have to take the pills. I can do the exercises by myself."

"Yes, but you won't."

I return to the living room and pretend to read the want ads. Ben begins supper, then out of the blue says, "Tell me more about Teresa Brancati."

I take a deep breath. "She's from Baltimore."

He stops slicing. "You told me that. I'm just wondering if maybe she'd be willing to stay with you a few hours each day."

I pause. "I don't think so, no."

"She's out of work, isn't she?"

"I just don't think she'd be interested." I turn a page of the newspaper.

"Would there be any harm in asking?"

"I think there would." I glance over at him. "I already asked. She said no."

"You already asked?"

"She said she wasn't a home health person. I think I offended her."

"Maybe you didn't approach her the right way. Do you think I should talk to her?"

"If anyone talks to her, it'll be me."

This is none of his business.

The next afternoon I stand on the Brancatis' doorstep holding the pot of chrysanthemums Ben brought home yesterday. I've carried it here under one arm, moving as carefully as possible.

"Hello, Mr. Whitaker," Teresa says, opening the door.

I hand her the plant and remove my cap. "This is for you."

"Thank you," she says, without enthusiasm. She's wearing the dark bathrobe again. "I didn't think you'd be coming."

"I wanted to talk to you."

"I don't think anything needs to be said."

She hasn't invited me in. I look past her.

"Pete and Ruby are at the mall."

"Ah. Perhaps you and I could sit for a minute. I have something I want to say."

She opens the door and motions toward the couch, looking uncertain. She perches on the front edge of Pete's recliner, pulls the robe down over her knees.

"First, I want to apologize," I say. "What I said was definitely wrong."

"I'm sure you meant it kindly," said Teresa.

"I didn't intend to hurt your feelings."

"Of course you didn't," she says, looking as if she hopes I'll change the subject, which I do.

"Teresa," I say.

She looks at me. I look back.

"Teresa, I want to ask you something?"

"Yes."

"Will you marry me?"

"I beg your pardon?"

"Will you marry me?"

She puts her hands to her temples. "This is another of your little jokes, isn't it?"

"I'm perfectly serious."

"Oh dear," she says. "Mr. Whitaker, of course I cannot marry you."

"Please call me Tom."

"Tom, of course I cannot marry you." She's trying to speak calmly, but her voice is quavering. I think she's tempted.

"Why can't you?" I ask, scooting forward a bit on the couch. "You're not married to someone else, are you?"

"Tom, I've known you for only a few days."

"I know that."

"And you're older than my father."

"I know that, too. I'd get down on one knee, Teresa, but I can't."

"Please stop. This is quite crazy." She stands and crosses to the fireplace.

"But you and I have such interesting conversations."

"Yes we do."

"And we could have so many more. And we both like old houses, and I have an old house. So I realized this morning, why shouldn't we get married? You need to make a change in your life. I'm too old for a long courtship."

"I'm sorry."

"I seem to have offended you again."

"I'm not offended, Mr. Whitaker. Tom. I'm just a little flustered. No one has ever proposed to me before. But no, the answer is no." She crosses to the kitchen. "Would you like some coffee? I can put on a fresh pot. And there's a little left of Ruby's date bread."

"I'm sorry to make such a mess of things," I say.

"No. It's all right."

We sit at the dining table where Snow White and the dwarfs hold hands in a circle.

"Let me suggest something," she says after a while. "If you'd like, I'd come down to your house for a few hours every day while your son's at work. Just as a friend. I could help you with your exercises if they aren't too complicated."

"Would you?" I say, dribbling coffee down my

chin. "I'd like that very much. It might be more than a few weeks. I'm hoping Stony Hill won't be ready."

"I'm not sure how long I'll be here either," she says, handing me a paper napkin. "But let's give it a try. The understanding has to be that you won't pay me."

"I understand."

"And you won't say anything more about getting married."

Coffee Cake

Every morning I fidget until she arrives. I worry she'll find something better to do with her time. Today, she's late, fifteen minutes late. She's never been late before. I'm sitting in the rocker and look over my shoulder to check the door, but I won't check again, because the door's ajar and she might come in and catch me looking anxious.

Roscoe hears her before I do, smells her probably, because his hearing is not as good as it used to be.

"Good morning, Tom," she says, stepping into the house.

The heaviness leaves my chest. "Good morning, Teresa."

"I'm sorry I'm late. I was on the phone with Mrs. Maynard. Nearly three weeks I've been here and the boxes with my clothes and other belongings hadn't come. So finally this morning, I called to find out what was going on, and she'd forgotten all about them. The boxes were still up in my room."

"How annoying," I say.

"She promised to send them today, but I don't trust her to remember." She takes off her jacket and hangs it in the closet.

"Anyway, look what I have for us." She's brought a dish covered in aluminum foil. "Sour-cream coffee cake."

Every morning Ruby sends Teresa down with something freshly baked. Ruby keeps half for herself and Pete. The rest comes here. Whatever it is, I have two of. I'm actually putting on weight.

Teresa starts a fresh pot of coffee. "Tell me how you're feeling," she asks across the counter. That's always her first question. Usually I say I'm fine but go on to complain about my feet and legs, which keep finding new ways to disappoint me. But this morning I've been so worried she wasn't coming I've forgotten about my body altogether. I actually can't remember how I'm feeling.

"Yesterday, it was your hip. How's your hip doing?"

"Yes, my hip," I say, looking down at it, trying to recall. When the coffee's ready, she returns with a tray.

Now will begin my favorite part of the morning: me telling stories over coffee and something sweet. I have so many stories, and, unlike Ben, she hasn't heard them before. She takes her usual seat opposite me, on the couch, a modern one with a back only half as high as it ought to be. I've urged her more than once to bring over a chair from the dining table, but she says she likes sitting straight up. She has excellent posture, especially for a woman her size. She's imposing even when sitting.

She pours coffee into china cups she found in Ben's cupboard. They came from his grandmother, I think—not my mother, his mother's mother, a woman who was not fond of me nor I of her. She found real napkins, too. It's only been a week and a half that she's been coming, but already she and I have customs. I like people who like customs.

Each day before she arrives, I think of a few stories I want to tell. I usually jot myself a note so I won't forget. This morning I've decided to tell one about my grandfather's twenty-year dispute with the property assessors. Just as I'm about to start, she says, "There's more to my conversation with Mrs. Maynard I need to tell you."

"Please," I say.

"Right after she promised to send the boxes, she whispered, 'Can I call you back?' I guessed right away that Mr. Maynard was in the room with her. All these years and she's still scared of him. And it's her money they live on.

"She called me back a few minutes later from her study and told me she wasn't doing so well without me. I'd been her calendar and her alarm clock, she said. Now she doesn't get anywhere on time. And she doesn't know where anything goes. And she hates having to deal with the gardener, who's hard of hearing, and with the dry cleaners and the housecleaners and what have you. She even hates deciding what the cook should fix for dinner, because she used to rely on me for suggestions. But what she said she missed most was our chatting about the children. So I asked how they were doing, because I do miss them. And she told me about Schuyler's first visit home from college. That's why I'm late. And when she finished, she completely surprised me. She asked if I'd be willing to come back."

"Come back?"

"And I said—because I knew she wouldn't be allowed to make the decision by herself—I said, what does Mr. Maynard think? And she said she hadn't talked to him, but she would if I'd be willing. I should have told her I'd think about it, but I said yes, right off."

"Don't go," I say. It just slips out.

"No?"

I fumble. "Don't go until you feel stronger. You need more rest."

I was right to be alarmed this morning. She's going to leave just when we're getting to know each other.

"You don't need to worry. Mr. Maynard will say no, and that will be the end of it. Mrs. M said she'd talk to him later this morning and call me back. I asked Ruby to give her the number down here if she calls. But she won't call."

Teresa takes another bite of coffee cake.

"How can you be so sure he'll say no if it means so much to Mrs. Maynard?"

"Because more happened between him and me after he fired me."

"Ah."

"I didn't leave right away. He said I could stay while I looked for a new job, but I was in such a daze for more than a week that I couldn't get started. Do you really want to hear?"

I nod.

"Finally, I called the agency that had placed me with the Maynards as a nanny back in 1985. I was so anxious I kept misdialing the number, but eventually I got through and made an appointment. Mrs. Underwood still runs the agency. I thought she'd take one look at me and say no family would hire a nanny who's over fifty and oversized and perspiring — it was in the 90s the afternoon I went to meet with her — but that's not what she said. What she said was that I wasn't a nanny anymore, that I was the head of staff for a fine, old home, a famous one. She picked up the phone, and, right while I sat there, set an interview for the next morning with a family who lived in Sandhurst, a gated community I'd never heard of. I didn't even know what a gated community was."

Unlike me, Teresa doesn't use her hands when she speaks. She sits quite still with her hands in her lap, talking evenly but intensely.

"The next morning I drove to the suburbs, and just when I thought I'd gotten lost I turned a corner and there was this big stone block with 'Sandhurst' carved into it. It looked like a tombstone. Just beyond the rock was a shed. I drove up and a guard in a uniform came out and asked who I was and called ahead for permission to let me in. Can you imagine? I felt like I was still living on an Army base.

"I drove around these curving streets until I found the house. It was huge, just as Mrs. Underwood had told me, huge but ugly. It had skinny, spindly pillars. The brick was too orangey, too uniform in color, the gravel in the semicircular driveway too white. In the front garden, pink and purple flowers were over here and yellow and orange ones were over there and red ones were all over and there were two fountains. Obviously, someone hadn't known when to stop. I took my foot off the brake and coasted away. I couldn't live in a place like that, not after the Lambert house.

"I trembled all the way home. I parked the car behind the house and avoided Mrs. M by climbing the back stairs to the third floor. That's where my rooms are. Were. Mr. Maynard always called it the attic, like I was some sort of bat. I threw myself on the couch in my sitting room. My chest was heaving. I was clammy. I had a headache.

She takes a second slice of coffee cake. "I shouldn't," she says. "I eat too much when I'm upset." She cuts a second slice for me.

"You can tell me the rest later, if you'd rather."

Chewing, she shakes her head and swallows. "I heard a knock at my door, but I didn't answer. I didn't want to talk to her. Instead, in walks Mr. Maynard. I nearly passed out. What was he doing barging into my room without being invited? Why was he home on a Friday morning anyway?

"'Mrs. Underwood just phoned,' he said. 'She wants to know why you didn't show up for the interview.' He was standing just this close to me. He smelled like an ashtray.

"I decided I had to face him then or never. 'Mr. Maynard,' I said. 'We need to talk right now.'

"'About what?' he said, as if he didn't know.

"'About why you're making me leave.'

"'I've explained to you before,' he said. 'The children are in college.'

"And I said, 'Why don't you tell the truth? The truth is you just don't like me, do you?'"

"'Mrs. Maynard and I are running late,' he said. 'We need to leave for the airport.'

"'Sit down, Mr. Maynard,' I told him. He didn't sit but I could tell he was listening. I shoved myself up from the couch in one move, which surprised us both. 'First of all, Mr. Maynard, you can't throw a person out of the home they've lived in for twenty-two years just because you don't like them.'"

Teresa's face has become more animated, her voice louder.

"'In fact, Mr. Maynard, I believe this really is more my home than yours. I'm the one who knows it. I'm the one who appreciates it. I'm the one who treats it with the respect it deserves. Just because you own it doesn't mean it's yours.'

"You said that?" I say.

"He was a bit shocked." She looks at me. "I'm sorry to make you listen to this, Tom."

"Go on," What a woman, I'm thinking.

She takes another bite. "So I took a step toward him and he took a step back and I kept talking. 'Now that I think of it,' I said, 'it would be fairer all around if you and Mrs. Maynard were the ones to move out.'

"'Calm down,' he said.

"'I'm perfectly calm,' I said, though, of course, I wasn't. 'There are plenty of other houses that would be quite suitable for you. You might consider looking in Sandhurst.'

"He took me by the shoulders and turned me so he could get past me out the door. 'If we weren't running late,' he said, 'I'd remove you from the house right this minute. Now call Mrs. Underwood and make up some excuse for this morning.'

"And with that he headed downstairs. I followed him to the landing and listened as he talked to Mrs. M, but I couldn't make out what he was saying, so I returned to the sitting room and stood at the window and watched as he backed out of the garage. Mrs. Maynard opened the passenger door and, as she stepped in, she looked up toward my window. I couldn't tell whether she saw me, but I stumbled backwards against the end of the couch and fell to the floor. That's when I started crying. I sobbed and sobbed. I sobbed even after I couldn't make any more tears. Dry heaves is what it felt like. Finally, I got up and walked across the hall into the storage room and dug around behind the Christmas decorations for my suitcases." Her eyes engage mine. "Oh dear. Here I've gone on and on. I'm sorry. All

I meant to do was tell you about Mrs. M's call. I'll bet you had a story ready, didn't you?"

"Finish your story," I say.

"I'm done. I called my father and told him I was coming to stay with him and Ruby." She folds her napkin and sits up straighter.

"I shouldn't want to go back to Baltimore, but I do." She stands and picks up our cups and dishes. "Why don't we take our walk now? It's supposed to cloud over."

"Don't you want to wait for Mrs. Maynard's call?"

"There's no point."

"You can't be sure. Maybe Mrs. Maynard will stand up to him."

Teresa looks over at the telephone, then nods slightly. "Well, actually, if it's all right with you, I would like to wait." She sits back down.

"We can take a walk later."

I feel virtuous. At the moment, I actually want Teresa to get what she desires. Or even better, I want a miracle: I want Mr. Maynard to apologize to her and beg her to come back and for her to say no.

We both sit silently, as if we expect the phone to ring at any moment. The house is quiet. I hear a tapping sound and look down and see that I'm drumming my fingers on the armrest.

Teresa reaches out to slice another piece of cake, then stops herself. "Dad and Ruby want me to stay. Dad's getting unsteady on his feet and Ruby's got emphysema. They could use my help. But I don't think I can do it. I shouldn't say this, but every time I walk into their living room and see Ruby's Little Mermaids and Donald Ducks and Dumbos, I think if I stay here much longer, I'll become an ordinary person again. Just an ordinary person. I wasn't an ordinary person at Lambert House."

"You are not an ordinary person, Teresa," I say. "You're not an ordinary person to me."

I reach across for her hand, but she sees my hand coming and pats it.

The Cupboard

Sometimes she'll be sitting there and I'll look over and ask myself, who is this woman, who is this solid, dark-haired woman? Could it be Anna Magnani? She'll look up. "It stopped raining," she'll say. Or "Are you getting hungry?" And then I'll know. It's Teresa. My wife.

Most afternoons you can find us in the living room. She knits or reads. I read or work the crossword. We don't talk a lot, but we're comfortable with the silences. Mealtimes are when we do our talking. It's still mostly me telling stories. She tells stories, too, though sad to say, I don't remember most of them a few minutes later. She doesn't seem to mind. I tell her her voice reminds me of my grandmother's. She tells me my stories remind her of her father's.

She's knitting me a cap now, not for outside but for sleeping, because she came in one morning and found me with my head under the pillow. She's using a blue yarn she says will go nicely with the pajamas she bought me for my birthday. Why she should care if the nightcap matches the pajamas I can't imagine — she's the only one who will ever see me in them — but she seems to care and that's what matters.

For over a month she came down to Ben's house every morning and stayed til early afternoon. We had our morning coffees and stories. We took walks along the horse-farm fence, fed carrots to the mare. She fixed us lunch. I taught her cribbage. I could have kept it up forever. Then Stony Hill called to say they had my unit ready. That's what they call it, a unit. Who'd want to live in a unit, when you can live in a home?

The very next weekend, Ben rented a U-Haul and drove us to Vermont to pick up the furniture I'd need in the apartment. Teresa came along. She wanted to see the farm. When we pulled into the driveway, I could see right off that she liked what she saw: the solid four-squareness of an old cape farmhouse. She faltered a bit when we stepped inside, shook her head when she saw the Frigidaire that was turning yellow, the water-stained wallpaper, the dog-scratched couch, but I said to her, "What this place needs is a woman's touch" and she gave me a look that suggested hers might be the touch it needed. I watched her examine the wainscoting in the dining room and the beams in the kitchen. She could see that the house has good bones. Seize the moment, I said to myself. So while Ben and a neighbor boy were upstairs dismantling my bed, I took her hand in mine. "Teresa," I said, "will you marry me?" "You weren't supposed to raise that subject again," she said, but in a tone that told me she was glad I had. "What do you say?" I asked. "My heart is pounding too hard to speak," she said. Mine too.

"You're an old fool," my sister Ellen said when I phoned her. "What was pounding was not her heart. That was opportunity knocking. Can't you see she wants your money, Tommy? She's a gold-digger." "Gold-digger!" I said. "Gold-diggers are blonde and slinky and thirty-five. Teresa's fifty-some and rather large." "It's a trade off," said Ellen. "She's not all that attractive. You're not all that rich."

What I should have said was, Ellen, face it, women have always married men for their money. Forty years ago, Claudia married me because she was raising two children on a schoolteacher's salary. Even today, pretty young women marry not-so-handsome doctors and bankers because they want to live well. It's the way of the world.

And anyway, I should have added, Teresa didn't marry me mostly for my money. She married me mostly for my house. Marrying me for my house isn't the same as marrying me for my money. The house really needs her. The whole farm needs her. I can't take care of it by myself anymore. I preserved it for my children and my children's children. And even though I now understand there will be no children's children, I still see myself as its guardian.

Ben could have had children, could still have children. Homosexuals have children. I've read about it in the paper. But he says he doesn't want children, says it as if not wanting them were an adequate reason for not having them. Well, I didn't much want children either, but when you're a young man and you marry a young woman they just happen.

Before I married Teresa, my plan, of course, was to will the place to Ben, even though he'd probably have decided to sell. He'll still be a young man when I die, still working in Connecticut. He probably couldn't afford two houses. Also, as far as I know, not many of his kind live up here. Now, everything will work out better. I'll pass the place on to Teresa. She'll care for it during her lifetime. And at her death many years from now, Ben will have retired and be in a position to move north. I've thought this all through. Sure, when Ben dies, the house and farm will pass out of the family. If it's like other places around here, someone from New York will buy it because they think it's charming. They'll replace the kitchen counters with granite slabs and add one of these family rooms with a phony fireplace. They'll boast that the house is old, but won't care who built it, won't know its stories.

I get a little obsessive on this subject, so maybe I should talk about something else. Before I do, though, here's the point: for now and for as long as possible, Teresa and I will live at the farm, here at home.

I'd hoped she and I could sleep together in my old room, but I can't climb the stairs anymore. They're too steep. My first day home, I stood at the bottom looking up in despair, like a child whose balloon has floated away. Teresa helped Ben move my bed and dresser into what used to be my study. Old Roscoe sleeps there with me. He can't climb anymore either. Right next to the study is a bathroom with a tub and shower that were added when my grandfather became as gimpy as I am.

Teresa sleeps right above me, in my old room. She bought a brass bed and an oak dresser at a house auction. Our arrangements aren't romantic — newlyweds on separate floors — but, at eighty-four, I'm glad to have my old bed, which is too small to share with an ample sized woman, and Teresa says she prefers a room of her own. She tucks me in at night, sits on the bed and chats before turning out my light. In the mornings, I get up early, as I've always done, putter around while the house is quiet. She stays up late and doesn't get up until seven.

Where my bed is isn't the only change. She took me at my word about the need for a woman's touch. She moved circumspectly, at least at first, waiting to feel at home, waiting for me to get used to her being around. The kitchen has been her most recent project. Until last month, it had the same linoleum it did when I first moved in. Serviceable, even if cracked and scuffed. But I told her she could replace it if she thought necessary, which she did. Under the old Frigidaire, she found a layer of even older linoleum. She pulled up some of that and at the bottom found wide pine boards, the ones my great-grandfather laid with his own hands. So that's what the floor is now, the original boards, sanded down and urethaned. And then she decided to replace the Frigidaire itself, which made me nervous, because I feared she'd buy one of these stainless steel things with the freezer compartment on the side and a spigot on the door that spits ice cubes. But she didn't. She picked a plain white one with the freezer on top, where it belongs. What's new around here isn't flashy.

I've come to realize — it's been a revelation — that she's a lot like my grandmother. Neither one of them born a Whitaker, but both with a destiny to become one, both of them practical and thrifty, and though a little humorless, not at all sour. Business-like, I'd call them. Teresa knows what's good for me, gives me my medicines with her home-cooked meals, makes sure I shave every couple of days, reminds me when the porch is icy. It's all right for women to be bossy about things that are good for their men.

She's sexy, too, if you'll pardon my saying so. If she's working next to me at the kitchen table, I'll put a hand on her hip, and she'll just let it stay there while she works. I like it best when she's kneading dough.

She massages my legs and hips on days when it's too cold for a walk. One day last week my leg cramped up when I got out of bed and she made me lie on my back. She rubbed my thigh and, would you believe, I got a sort-of erection. She looked a little surprised, as if she were seeing a cat standing on its hind legs, but she didn't stop rubbing.

Teresa. Teresa. Te-Re-Sa.

I'm in love. For lunch today, I made her a grilled-cheese sandwich.

Which brings me nearly up to the present, to this afternoon actually. I'm waking from my nap and hear noises from the kitchen. They're not cooking noises. They're the ominous rumble of things being rearranged.

I trudge out to see what's going on, not even going to the bathroom first.

"I have something to show you," she says. "I've moved the glasses and mugs to the cupboard on the other side of the sink."

I'm speechless.

Suddenly, too much is different.

Suddenly, the kitchen feels like someone else's.

First she replaced the linoleum and the ice box. Then she made curtains for the windows even though they didn't really need them. Then she had the walls painted yellow, which is the color she says they used to be under several other layers, but isn't the color it's been for as long as I can remember. And now this. She's changed what's inside the cupboards. Once you start changing the insides, you're really reaching substance.

"You look upset," she says.

"I am not upset," I snarl.

"I'm glad," she says, even though she can surely tell I didn't mean it. "I've put the glasses right here over the dishwasher so they'll be easier for me to unload. I switched the canned goods to where the glasses were."

"That's quite a change," I say.

"Tom, you and I talked about this yesterday."

That's a line she's used once too often: "You and I talked about this yesterday."

"And what did I say?"

"You said you liked it the way it was, and I said I really needed it and you said, okay."

"And you took that for a yes?" I lean on my cane, swaying. "The glasses have been in the south cupboard since my grandmother's time."

"Your grandmother didn't have a dishwasher that had to be emptied."

"I'll open up the cupboard looking for a glass and end up holding a can of vegetable soup."

She puts her dishcloth on the counter. "Okay. Do you want me to put the dishes back where they were?" Her tone is not appeasing. It contains an unfamiliar hint of challenge.

"As a matter of fact, yes," I say. "Put them back. Put them back right now."

"Tom, I'm getting angry. You're acting foolish."

I slam my cane down on top of the counter.

She doesn't even flinch. "Sit down, Tom. Your face is bright red. You're rocking back and forth. You'll have a heart attack."

She looks concerned, which makes me concerned. I sit.

"Now," she says, "sit still. I'll make us some tea."

"No."

"Do you want a glass of water?"

"No."

Calm down, I tell myself. Remember: without her, you'd be living at that sanitarium. You'd be eating three meals a day with strangers who talk about their bowel movements. It's your own fault she made the curtains, bought the new icebox, painted the walls. You encouraged her. Of course, if she'd been sufficiently sensitive to your feelings, she'd have anticipated the cumulative effect.

In front of me, both cupboard doors stand open. I look inside the one where she's moved the canned goods. I see right off that she's done more than switch cupboards.

"No," I say, outraged all over again, "No, no, no. Soups go on the bottom shelf. The beans and spaghetti and rice go on the next shelf up."

"Tom," she says, her eyes in slits. "It's more convenient for me this way. What I use most is more reachable."

"Me. Me. Me. All you think about is me. This is still my house, you know. This is still my house."

She stands, arms crossed, without speaking, probably waiting for me to back off, to apologize, to do something. But I don't. She takes several breaths and waits some more, then turns and walks into the back hall, comes back with her coat. "Your house and welcome to it," she says, whisking the keys off the kitchen counter.

"Where are you going?" I grab the door to keep her from slamming it behind her.

"Goodbye," she says.

She walks down the steps and starts the car, not looking back.

"Where are you going?"

She drives off in the direction of the village, in the direction of Connecticut actually. The taillights disappear around the bend. The afternoon is already fading.

"I haven't had my medicines," I shout in her wake.

Most married men my age have had the same wives for fifty or sixty years. They know how to argue with each other. They know what stomping out means, what driving away means. I don't know anything about this woman.

I peer out the front window. The car doesn't return. I look around. "Roscoe," I say. He doesn't respond. He's almost completely deaf now. Except when eating or peeing, he dozes on his pad in my bedroom. I look at the clock on the stove. It's way past his normal feeding time. Teresa was irresponsible to leave without feeding him.

I hobble into the bedroom. "Roscoe," I say loudly, rubbing his flank with my cane. He opens his eyes and stirs. "How about some supper?"

He tries to get up, but his hips fail him and he falls back on his haunches. Teresa can lift him, but I can no longer do it by myself.

"Try again, Roscoe."

He just lies back down. I think maybe if I sit next to him, I can get him started. I take a pillow off the bed and drop it next to his pad. Then, leaning on the mattress with one elbow, I lower myself onto the pillow and sit. I put my hands under his hips. "Here we go," I say. But I can't get enough leverage to budge him. I try again, fail again. So I stay there and rub his back, scratch his ears. "I'll take care of you," I say, leaning against the frame of the bed.

Daylight dims to black. The bedside clock provides the only illumination: matchstick numbers of incandescent red. I could pull myself up and turn on a lamp, but I don't want to get up more than once and Roscoe needs my company, so I remain where I am.

Where is that woman anyway?

Down the road lives an old man named Otto Grimmer. He's even older than I am, must be over ninety. He lives with his son Axel and Axel's wife Lydia. Axel's the one who nearly froze to death when he fell into the feeding trough. Every sunny morning, even in January, old Otto sits on the lawn in one of those molded plastic chairs watching the cars and the birds and the squirrels. He was out there yesterday when Teresa and I drove into the village, him bundled up, wearing his orange hunting cap, false teeth out, grinning, looking like a jack-o-lantern. Teresa honked, but I don't think he's able to see well enough to know who it was. He waved anyway. He's contented. Well loved. A lucky fellow. Lydia takes care of him, fine care of him. That's the point. She's a good woman.

I should have moved into that nursing home in

Connecticut. If I had, I wouldn't be sitting here on the floor. If I had, the cook wouldn't walk out right at meal time.

After my grandmother voted for Roosevelt for the third time, my grandfather said women should never have been given the vote. Grandmother didn't know her proper boundaries. That's what he told her. You don't know your boundaries.

Suddenly it's pitch black. The electricity's gone off. The clock goes blank and disappears. We get power outages often here. They rarely last long, except after blizzards. But sometimes they last for whole days.

This house, this farm. They're too much of a burden. Trespassers built a whole house on my land, and I didn't even know. And there's more than just the trespassers. There's the fungus that's killing the hemlocks. And rising taxes and rising heating bills. And the leaky roof in the barn.

The electricity comes back on. But now the red light on the clock is flashing. It'll keep on flashing until someone resets the time. It's like sharing a room with a traffic blinker. I shut my eyes, but I can still see the pulsing glow. One of my feet falls asleep.

Maybe it's time to sell.

"Teresa," I shout. "Where are you?"

Roscoe raises his head.

"She's gone," I tell him.

After a while, I hear a car pull into the driveway. The kitchen door opens and she calls my name, sounding alarmed, which she should be.

"What's wrong?" she says when she finds me. "Why are you sitting on the floor in the dark?"

"As you can see, I'm keeping Roscoe company. He needed me. And he's hungry. He needs to be fed."

"He's already been fed, Tom. I fed him during your nap."

"Oh."

She puts an arm under my elbow and pulls me up, me so stiff my leg won't straighten out. She holds me steady until I'm able to walk.

In the kitchen, she fixes us a supper of scrambled eggs and toast. I want more than eggs and toast, but she doesn't ask and I don't say anything.

"I need you," I say.

"You're a little crazy, Thomas Whitaker."

"I know."

More silence.

"Where did you go?" I ask eventually.

"To the grocery."

"We went this morning, didn't we?"

"I went again. I took a grocery cart and walked every aisle. I filled it with all the things I'm not supposed to eat, filled it all the way up until it mounded over the top and left it in the bakery section next to a table of chocolate cakes."

"That's a little crazy."

"It isn't like me."

"Did you have a good time?"

"No. Not really."

We're quiet again. We stay quiet right through cleaning up. I help a little, leaning against the stove wiping the stove top.

Now it's late, close to my bedtime. We've moved to the living room. We're often quiet in here, happy but quiet, but tonight the quiet isn't happy. It's the quiet when you're listening for a burglar. Teresa's knitting. She looks cross, but maybe she's just concentrating. I try working the crossword. "What's a five-letter word for 'thin cotton fabric,' first letter 'v'?" I say, forgetting I wasn't going to bother her.

"Voile," she says.

"V-w-a-l-l?" I say.

"V-o-i-l-e," she says. She doesn't say more. I look over wondering what she's thinking. Usually she looks back when I look at her, but not this time. "The new curtains in the kitchen are voile," she says at last. "During the day, you can see sunlight through them." I'm still looking at her. She has a tiny smile on her face.

The Cemetery

Cold feet. Cold from the inside out. Cold in a way that blankets can't warm, so far are they from my inadequate heart. I've gotten used to them. But what I can't get used to is that I've started waking up some mornings and can't feel my feet at all. I can locate them only from memory. I pull back the sheet, and, lo, they're staring at me, gnarled and veiny, unfeeling. I dangle them over the edge of the bed until they begin to prickle, rest them on the floor until they feel solid enough to put weight on.

These are the same feet that, when I was twenty-three, hiked the Long Trail from end to end, the same feet that, well into my seventies, climbed the hill behind the house without complaint. For all they did for me, I never thanked them. And now it's too late. It's made me grateful for what I've still got—my eyes, for example, which need glasses for reading but not for watching the news; even my elbows, under-appreciated joints, which bend far more willingly than my knees.

This morning my feet are more remote than ever. I'm sitting on the side of the bed and they've moved from numb to tingling, but the tingling doesn't go away. I'd hoped for better, because Ben is here, and after breakfast he and Teresa and I plan to visit the cemetery where the Whitakers are buried. I'll have to walk a fair ways within the cemetery.

Only two spaces remain in the Whitaker plot. One is for me. The other I'd always assumed would be for Ben, but now will go to Teresa. I worried that Ben would resent the change of plans, but when I raised it with him, he didn't seem to care. He claimed he'd never given any thought to where he'd be buried, or even whether he'd be buried at all. Perhaps he was just being diplomatic.

While I wait for my feet, I hear murmurs of Ben's and Teresa's voices coming from the kitchen. Over the past year, they've become good friends, despite having been leery of each other at first. Ben was leery of Teresa because he thought she must have very poor judgment to marry someone like me. Teresa was leery of Ben because she could tell what Ben was thinking. Neither told me that, but I think that's what was going on. Fortunately, I've provided them a common cause. Now, when Ben calls and Teresa answers the phone, he sometimes doesn't even ask to talk to me.

Eventually, my feet come around and I slog through the dining room to the kitchen. Ben, who arrived last night after I'd gone to bed, gives me a hug and we exchange how-are-yous and you're-looking-wells. Actually, he really is looking well this morning, the best he's looked in quite some time. He's started going to a gymnasium several times a week. And he's just returned from a beach vacation with a new friend he met at the gymnasium. Usually on the Saturdays he visits, he puts on the tattered overalls and boots that he leaves here, but this morning he's wearing a white dress shirt and fresh khakis.

"I was about to get you up," Teresa says. "I think we should go soon. It's supposed to rain later in the morning."

I peer out the kitchen window at a sky of mid-gray clouds, darker to the west.

"I can be ready in a few minutes," I say. "I'll just get dressed."

"You need breakfast and a shower first," she says, "We're not in that big a hurry. A bowl of cereal won't take but a few minutes."

"But…"

"Sit," she orders, but jocularly.

By the time I've dressed, the sky has brightened a bit, still overcast but not threatening. Ben lifts Roscoe into the back seat of the car and scoots in beside him. Teresa drives. Roscoe's hairs coat the floor of the car, cling to the upholstery. I usually don't notice, but today I'm wearing dark pants.

"So," Teresa asks as we set out, "tell me more about the Whitakers I'm going to meet."

"I'll tell you when we get there." I say. "But I'll tell you now about two who ought to be there but aren't. My parents."

"Really?"

"They're buried down in Concord."

"Oh yes, of course."

"It's not 'of course.' They should have been buried here. There was room for them. It hurt my grandmother's feelings when Dad bought a plot in Concord."

"So why did he?" Ben asks from the back seat.

"I'm not sure."

"Didn't he get along with his parents?"

"Of course, he got along with his parents. What a thing to say. I think he just came to think of Concord as home. He'd lived there ever since college. And my mother was from New Hampshire, remember. I also don't think he ever liked being way out in the country. He had allergies. Everything made him stuffed up. Dust in the barn. Grass pollen. Mold. He'd drive us up here on Labor Day when I was a boy and start sneezing before he even got out of the car. Gram would make all his favorite foods, but he'd still be miserable. She always cooked something special for me, too, when I was little, even did it for you in her nineties when you were little. She'd make you macaroni and cheese, with real cheddar. Do you remember?"

"No," Ben says. "I was only five when she died."

"Weren't you older than that? It seems to me you were older."

"No, five. I do remember that she was quite large. I also remember the wart on her chin."

"You'll have to talk a little louder," I say.

"I said I remember the wart on her chin."

"Now that's a peculiar thing to remember. Besides, it wasn't a wart. It was a mole."

Ben says nothing.

"Once when you came up, she'd made you a stuffed pony on the sewing machine and you took it to bed with you every night."

"Really? That's nice. I don't remember."

"Five is plenty old enough to remember a stuffed animal."

"One thing I do remember is not being permitted to go to her funeral. You made me stay at the farmhouse with Mrs. Wattles."

"I did?"

"Yes, you said that funerals were no place for children."

"Well they aren't. Gram had an open casket."

"Children need to learn about death," he says. This is an old wound.

"You'd probably have pointed at her mole," I add. This wonderful woman, and all he remembers is a mole.

"Well," he says, shifting to a lighter tone, "you have to admit, the mole was interesting. It had little hairs growing out of it."

"Now, stop," I say.

The cemetery is on a dirt road. Teresa pulls up in front, parking as close as she can to the gate, which is rusted open now, no longer needed to keep out cows. Not even people come here anymore. Not many anyway. Most folks who are buried here have been dead so long no one's left who misses them.

Those who are still missed are buried in the new cemetery beyond the golf course.

I use both hands to lift my legs out of the car. I fear they'll buckle when I put weight on them, but Ben gives me a hand and I grip the top of the door to steady myself. I'm determined to make this work. With Ben on one side and Teresa on the other—just one of them would have been sufficient—I make it up the three stone steps to the level area where the graves are. We leave old Roscoe dozing in the car.

"Oh, my stars," says Teresa, looking toward the east.

There's no better view in town than from right here. Teresa's looking toward Mount Moosilauke. Actually, with the low clouds, today's view is nearer, the mountain obscured, but you can still make out overlapping rows of distant hills, some topped with fog, and below us the Connecticut River snaking south. The town fathers knew they'd spend many more years dead than alive, so they wanted something fine to look at.

We stand for a few minutes and admire the prospect. Leaning on my cane, my footing is secure. "The Whitakers are down there and over," I say, starting towards the back of the cemetery, which is really the front, if you think of the front as facing the view. I read aloud the names on some of the markers we pass. "Randall," I say, "That's the Randall of Randall's Pharmacy and Randall & Cooper, the lawyers. And the McGuires. They owned one of the big farms on the road to Windsor."

Nearly all the stones are small and unassuming until we come to the Fowlers, where each generation tried to outdo the one before. The biggest stone belongs to Ed Fowler, who died not that long ago. It's a granite pillar a story and a half tall, with a ball at the top, and his name on the side in an arc of gothic letters. "Edward Fowler," I say and point to the pillar. "That's just what you'd have expected of him."

"Which is what?" says Teresa.

"Something pretentious. He drove a white Lincoln, the only Lincoln in the village, maybe the only Lincoln in Vermont."

As we go along, Ben picks up empty beer cans and carries them over to a trash barrel. Teenagers' droppings. Nothing changes. Eventually, we reach the Whitakers. Three rows of six graves each. The family gravestones are slender and upright, of identical size, the men's and women's alike, with simple lettering. The only extra flourish on any of them is the symbol of the Grand Army of the Republic on my great-grandfather's stone. His is the first one in the first row, the beginning. I clear my throat and read aloud.

"Daniel Whitaker, August 22, 1842–December 8, 1908, and next to him, Catherine Holliday Whitaker, October 13, 1846 - May 14, 1901. Your great-great-grandparents, Ben. Daniel's father was a farmer down in Massachusetts who didn't have a lot of land, so Daniel moved to Vermont in the

1850s. Why he didn't move west, beyond the Appalachians, across the Mississippi even, where the soil was better, I do not know, but he chose to move here. He joined the Union army when war broke out and was injured twice, once seriously, a bullet in the thigh at Spotsylvania. They sent him home with a bad leg he limped on for the rest of his life. Down over there are the Hollidays." I point to the opposite corner of the cemetery. "Daniel married Elijah Holliday's daughter, Catherine. Elijah loaned Daniel the money to buy the farm, which was a piece of someone else's, and Daniel and Catherine cleared more land and built the farmhouse."

I move a few paces to my right along the row. "Daniel and Catherine had five children. These two are Nancy and Jeremiah, who died, you see, when they were infants. Then comes my grandfather, Thomas Holliday Whitaker, and my grandmother Lucy Williams Whitaker."

"I'm impressed that you remember all these names," says Teresa.

"Me too," I say. I point toward Thomas's stone. "See. He was born on May 26 and died on May 26, on his 81st birthday."

"I read somewhere," says Ben, "that many people die on or right after their birthdays, more than you'd expect by chance."

"Is that so?" says Teresa.

Ben nods. "The article said maybe it's because if an old person is failing near the time of his birthday, he's likely to try to hold on until he becomes one year older."

"My birthday's coming up," I say.

"Yes," says Ben, "but you're not failing. You'll live to a hundred."

"Now what was I talking about?" I ask.

"Your grandfather," says Teresa.

"Oh, yes, my grandfather. Well I don't need to tell you stories about him, do I, or my grandmother? I've told you so many. Except I will say that Granddaddy, even though he was a gruff old codger, liked me a lot, better than any of the other grandchildren, I think. Of course, maybe he made each of the grandchildren feel that way. He was the one who taught me to hunt, and split wood, and grow corn and tomatoes, everything I know about the outdoors, except for wildflowers and birds, which my grandmother taught me."

I stand silently for a moment. I'm sure I will never visit here again. I feel a certain awe these days when I realize I'm doing something for the last time. Just last Sunday, Teresa and I drove down to the fire department's chicken barbeque. I've gone every year for thirty-some years. I was standing there talking to the fire chief and had this strong sense that this would be my last one. I didn't feel sad. I felt grateful that I recognized the significance of the moment, oddly like doing something important for the first time, since you can't repeat the first time either.

I've just noticed that Teresa is gripping my elbow. Maybe I've been wobbling without knowing it. Or maybe she believes I'm struggling with my emotions, which is actually not true, but nice of her to feel.

"Tom," she says. "Look in the third row." She's pointing to the far right corner of our plot.

I look up. She doesn't need to tell me what she's seen. Only one space is left where there ought to be two. One, two, three, four, five tombstones. Five in a row that only holds six. And a newish stone on the fifth one. I can't believe my eyes.

I step past Gram's grave, stepping faster than I ought to, feeling a flash of pain in my hip. The three of us move toward the grave of the intruder.

Michael Rhoads Whitaker, January 8, 1915 - November 16, 1997.

"Good lord," I say. "I didn't remember Michael was here."

"Who was Michael, Dad?"

"He was dad's brother William's son. William's there in the second row. I didn't remember Michael was dead. If you'd asked, I'd have guessed he still lived in New York. I'm shocked he got here without my knowing. Of course, I probably did know. I probably just forgot." I stand there trying to get my bearings. "I never knew him very well. He was nine years older than me. He went off to New York City after he finished school and rarely came back. But you'd think I'd remember his funeral."

"His funeral was probably in New York," says Ben.

"I suppose. He never amounted to much, I don't think. He left here to become an actor but ended up working in a department store. I heard he did window displays. And here he is taking Teresa's spot." I shouldn't speak ill of the dead, but I'm annoyed at the situation, at my lapse of memory.

Ben looks pensive. "I don't remember you're ever mentioning him."

"So what are we going to do?" I say.

Teresa is unruffled. "I think the answer is easy. You should be buried here with your grandmother and grandfather. I'd always planned to be cremated."

"A woman should be buried next to her husband."

Ben looks up. "What if we combined the two infants into a single grave? Then we could move a few other bodies to open up two places in this row."

"Do they let you do things like that?" I say.

"We can find out," he says. "Actually, maybe we wouldn't even have to move any bodies. We could leave the bodies where they are and just move a few stones. Who would ever know?"

"Don't be disgusting," I say.

The pain in my hip has become more intense. I need to sit. With Teresa's help, I settle a few feet away on a chair-height stone in the plot next to ours. I watch Ben as he stands in front of Michael's grave.

"This is such a peaceful place," says Teresa, a comment that might have been appropriate a few minutes ago, but certainly isn't now. "We'll have to come back again on a sunny day."

"I don't think so," I say.

"On Monday, I'll call whoever's in charge," says Ben, coming over to us, "and find out about moving graves."

"I still don't believe it," I say. "I was so certain there were two spots. I've never seen Michael's stone, I'm sure of that. Is it possible I haven't been here in a dozen years?"

I feel disrespectful sitting on someone's tombstone, but I don't trust my legs enough yet to get up. Teresa stands next to me with a hand on my shoulder. Ben revisits the rows of Whitakers, reading the names to himself, then returns to stand in front of Michael's grave. Eventually, I feel strong enough to try moving. "Shall we go?"

"If you're ready," says Ben. He and Teresa help me up. Ben holds my elbow as we move slowly toward the car.

"What more can you tell me about Michael?" he asks.

"Not very much."

"Do you know if he ever married or had children?"

"I don't think he did, no."

"Did it ever occur to you, Dad, that he was probably gay?

I pause. "I thought maybe that was what you were thinking. I don't remember whether I ever thought that or not. Everyone said he was artistic, but he seemed, you know, normal enough."

Ben doesn't speak.

"I don't mean as opposed to abnormal. I mean he seemed ordinary."

Ben still doesn't speak.

"You know what I mean."

He shakes his head in a sort of shrug.

"Ben, I'm old. You're going to have to take me the way I am." We walk a few steps. "I love you. That has to be enough."

He smiles slightly. "I suppose it is. It'll have to be."

We approach the steps to the car. I'd hoped to feel strong enough to descend on my own, but Teresa and Ben see that I can't and each takes an elbow. They ease me down. Lift me down, actually.

"We're just a few steps from the car," says Ben.

"I'm all right," I say. "I'm just ready to be home."

Tomatoes

Teresa stands outside the stall while I take a shower. I'm able to soap my chest and face and underarms and private parts, can wash my hair if she squeezes shampoo onto my scalp, but she has to do my legs and shoulders and back, while I hold onto the railings. Since the strokes, I can't grip tightly.

Stroke is too strong a word for what I had, the doctor said. He prefers "mini-stroke," but I say, call a stroke a stroke. The first time, Teresa heard a gurgling sound coming from the living room. She found me leaning against a window. She couldn't understand what I said to her. And five minutes later, though I felt better, I couldn't remember what I'd tried to say. The doctor put me on blood thinners to prevent a bigger stroke, but I've had two more small ones since, each lasting a bit longer than the one before. After each one I feel more frustrated and more frail. I'm using a walker most of the time now, particularly in the early mornings. The best I can do then is inch along, stooped, head down as if I were looking for something.

Teresa towels me off while I sit on the stool we

keep in the bathroom. I look down at my gray-blue skin as she dries my neck. This isn't fair to her. We've been together less than two years.

"What do you want to wear today?" she asks.

"I think I'll just put on fresh pajamas and stay in my robe."

"We're going to the veterinarian's, remember. So you'll need to get dressed."

I think for a moment. "Would you mind going alone?"

Roscoe died a few weeks ago, during the night on his pad next to my bed. He woke me up whimpering, but I went back to sleep and in the morning he was gone. Teresa and I took him to be cremated. We planned to go back today to pick up his ashes.

She sits on the toilet lid and clips my nails.

"I have something I want to discuss," I say. "I want to talk to you about my body."

"Where does it hurt?"

"Not that body. I want to talk about my body after it's dead. What to do with it."

"Now Tom, that's all settled. You and I are going to be buried with your parents down in Concord."

"No we're not. That was a terrible plan."

"But it was your idea, since we couldn't both be buried in the cemetery here."

"Well, I have a new plan."

"Let's get you into your bathrobe first," she says. She often talks to me this way now, the way she would to a child.

"No," I say. "Now."

"All right." She puts down the nail scissors.

"The plan is this. You and I are going to be buried with Roscoe in the orchard."

"What?"

"We're going to bury Roscoe's ashes in the orchard."

"Yes."

"Well, then we'll bury ourselves there, too. Our caskets. We'll have stones made for us just like the ones for the other Whitakers. That way you and I can be together, in Vermont."

Teresa wrinkles her nose. "What a ghoulish idea, being buried in your own yard." She wipes her hands on my towel and stands up. "Besides, I'm sure they don't let people do that. You can't just bury people in your lawn."

"In the orchard. And it's my orchard."

"Well, whatever the law is, I won't agree to it."

"I think we should think about it."

"I'll think about it, but I doubt that I'll change my mind. Let's finish getting you dressed."

After breakfast, she leaves for the veterinarian. I realize almost immediately that I should have gone with her. I'm upset about our argument. I'm missing Roscoe. I think this is the first time I've been alone in the house without him. I pick up yesterday's paper to work the crossword. A few months ago I started making too many mistakes, so I gave up using a pen. This morning I have trouble pulling up words at all, so I put the paper aside and snooze on the sofa. Eventually, Teresa returns home bearing Roscoe's remains in a container barely large enough to hold one of his old tennis balls. I'm amazed. So much dog—an entire Springer spaniel—in such a small box. But the box is handsome, a dark cherry cube with "Roscoe" on the lid, and I ask her to put it—him—in the bookcase, next to his photograph. When Ben comes up next, we'll bury the box at the base of my favorite tree, the Cortland I most liked to climb as a boy.

"You know," I say over lunch, still thinking about Roscoe. "I have another idea. Instead of burying us in the orchard, we could be cremated and just bury the ashes there."

Teresa perks up. "I didn't think you'd consider cremation."

"I wouldn't, but it's better than the alternatives."

"I think it's worth considering."

"And it would save money."

I watch idly out the kitchen window. We had an inch of snow yesterday, our first sticking snow of the season. It's still November, so most of it has already melted, but small clumps are holding on. I want to bury Roscoe before the ground freezes. One February long ago, I buried one of Gram's barn cats up on the hillside and had to use a pick ax. Of course, this time there's no rush. It's not as if Roscoe will start smelling. But I'd like to get him settled. I want to do right by him.

We linger at the kitchen table after lunch, reading the morning paper. A photo of a dog catching a Frisbee reminds me of Roscoe when he was young, and I feel sad again. A dark bird, probably a starling, lands on the vegetable bed. I watch it march around, poke its beak into the soil, ruffle its feathers. "Teresa."

"Yes." She looks up.

"I have a different idea."

"So many ideas in one day. I can hardly keep up with you."

"I want half my ashes buried in the orchard, but the other half I want you to use to fertilize the tomatoes."

Her brow creases and she turns and looks out the window.

"Ash is rich in calcium," I say. "I've been taking calcium tablets all these years, so my bones should be full of it." I pause and wait for a reaction. "Teresa."

She looks at me. "Sorry."

"You'll need to be careful with the ashes. Ash is — what do you call it? It could burn the new leaves. Alkaline. Ashes are alkaline. You'll want to spread it several weeks before transplanting the seedlings."

"I see."

"Now remember, you need to start the first seeds indoors in early March. Granddaddy always started them on the fifteenth."

I take a sip of coffee. "'Beware the Ides of March,' my grandmother always said, because from mid-March on, Granddaddy would be focused on his tomatoes. Actually, you have to start even before

March, of course, because in January, you have to sit down with the seed catalogs."

She nods.

"You'll want to check out the new varieties, maybe even order one or two. Over the years, my favorites have always been the Jet Stars, because they thrive this far north, and Early Girls, because they ripen a week or two before the Jet Stars. And Sweet 100's for cherry tomatoes. Jet Stars, Early Girls, Sweet 100's. Those are the ones I'd order if I were you."

She nods again. I have a feeling I've told her all this before.

"During the second week of March, you fill twenty or so of the little peat pots with a starter mix. Jiffy Mix is good. Then you place two seeds in each pot, one in the center and one off to the side. I always used a pencil eraser to make the seed hole. You push down only a quarter inch or so, just so there's room enough for the seed." I illustrate by touching the surface of my coffee with a fingertip. She nods once again.

"Then immerse each peat pot in warm water up to the rim, so the pot gets wet enough that it won't pull the water out of the planting mix. Pack the pots together tightly in the aluminum pan that's on the shelf by the water heater and cover the pan with plastic. Clear plastic. From then til they germinate, they need to be in a warm place like the pantry, not too cool but not too warm, and you have to check every day to make sure they're moist enough." I stop. She doesn't seem to be listening.

"You know," I say, "don't you think it would be a good idea to take some notes?"

She hesitates, then fetches a tablet and pen from my desk.

I sit upright and go back over everything I've said, adding more details. I instruct her when to remove the plastic and place the pan of seedlings under the fluorescent lights in the storage room. And how to transfer the baby plants into milk cartons and when to transplant the young plants into the garden.

She writes everything down. I see her draw arrows when I remember something I should have said earlier. My voice feels stronger as I go along. I take her through the entire summer regimen of spraying, watering and weeding and end with a list of neighbors who've always appreciated a gift of the ripe fruit. The last on the list is Eleanor Klinck, who's especially fond of the Early Girls. I'm so pleased with my performance I can't help rubbing my hands together in satisfaction. Teresa claps. Yesterday, I couldn't come up with my own telephone number, but today I can recall every detail of the life cycle of the tomato.

And then I remember about Eleanor Klinck. "Wait a moment," I say. "Didn't Eleanor die last year?"

"Yes."

"Why didn't you say something?"

"It didn't seem important."

"You just didn't want me to feel foolish, did

you? Now I feel even more foolish. I was feeling so good."

"For heaven's sake. You should still feel good, re-membering so much." She gets up from her chair. "You know what? Let's take a walk."

"Now?"

"You're doing so well today. Let's go out into the garden. You haven't been out to check since I put it down for the winter."

"Do you think I can get there?" The ground is uneven. I'm fearful of tipping over, even with the walker.

"I'll bet you can."

I put a hand on the seat of the chair and push my-self up. Haltingly but without her help, I roll the walker across the kitchen floor and into the back hall. Teresa holds my coat, and I work my arms through the sleeves. I must look peculiar wearing a jacket over my bathrobe, but she and I are the only ones here.

"It's turning into a fine day," she says. "You al-ways liked Novembers."

November and July and August. They're my fa-vorites, but November is the only one that isn't on every other Vermonter's list of favorites. In Novem-ber before the heavy snows, you can walk through the woods and see so much more than you can when the leaves are out, see the trunks of trees re-ceding up the hillsides. And there are always a few warm days, days you can be out without even a jacket, the last warm days before winter.

She opens the back door onto the porch. I look up the hillside toward the ridge. Even at midday, the low autumn sun casts long shadows. I edge myself outside. Last year, Ben built a simple wood ramp from the porch to the ground. I scoot myself along it, fearful the walker will get away from me. Teresa stands beside the ramp, ready to stop me. At the bottom, I pause to catch my breath, then cross the lawn, edging the wheels over the dips. I stop beside the tomato bed.

"It's good we came out," I say. "I remember something else I need to tell you. Have we talked about rotating?" She smiles gently. I'm sure I've told her before, but she's inviting me to tell her again. "You shouldn't plant the tomatoes in the same spot two years in a row. You should use a three-year rotation. Greens one year, beans and peas the next, tomatoes the third. Plant the tomatoes over there next year." I point to the bed where spinach, chard, and kale grew a few months before.

The garden has been put away for winter, leaf mulch worked carefully into the soil. "Did I do this?"

"No, I did," she says, "but you told me what to do."

"You're good."

"I'm learning."

I chose the right woman, didn't I?

We stand quietly. She pulls her sweater more tightly around her.

"Are you getting chilled?" I ask.

"A little. I should have worn a jacket."

"Here, take mine." I lift my hands from the walker.

"Don't be silly. I'll be okay."

"Go back in before you catch cold. I'd like to stay out a few more minutes."

"I'll stay, too, unless you want some time by yourself."

"No, stay."

I edge the walker closer to her.

"You know," she says after a while, "I am getting cold." She squeezes my hand and turns toward the house. "I'll watch from the window and help you in when you're ready."

"Don't," I say. "I think I can make it by myself."

David Chambers grew up in Indiana and taught for over thirty years at the University of Michigan Law School. Since the turn of the century, he has lived in Vermont, writing fiction. *The Old Whitaker Place* is his first novel.

Other titles in the Miami University Press fiction series:

Under the Small Lights | John Cotter
The Guide to the Flying Island | Lee Upton
A Fight in the Doctor's Office | Cary Holladay
Badlands | Cynthia Reeves
The Waiting Room | Albert Sgambati
Mayor of the Roses | Marianne Villanueva

To see our complete catalog of poetry and fiction, please visit www.muohio.edu/mupress.